THE INHERITANCE

A REVERSE HAREM ROMANCE

MIKA LANE

HEADLANDS PUBLISHING

COPYRIGHT

Copyright© 2018 by Mika Lane
Headlands Publishing
4200 Park Blvd. #244
Oakland, CA 94602

The Inheritance is a work of fiction. Names, characters, (most) places, and incidents are either the product of the author's creativity or are used fictitiously. Any resemblance to actual persons, living or dead, events, or locales is entirely coincidental.

All rights reserved. This book or any portion thereof may not be reproduced or used in any manner whatsoever without the express written permission of the publisher except for the use of quotations in a book review.

CONTENTS

Copyright	1
25% off coupon	5
1. Garnet	6
2. Nathaniel "Nat"	11
3. Garnet	17
4. Lincoln "Linc"	25
5. Garnet	30
6. Baldwin "Win"	38
7. Garnet	45
8. Ambrose "Brose"	52
9. Garnet	60
10. Nat	67
11. Garnet	74
12. Linc	82
13. Garnet	89
14. Win	97
15. Garnet	105
16. Brose	111
17. Garnet	117
18. Nat	124
19. Garnet	131
20. Win	139
21. Garnet	144
22. Brose	149
23. Garnet	156
24. Nat	162
25. Garnet	167
26. Win	175
27. Garnet	181
28. Brose	187

29. Garnet	193
30. Garnet	197
About the Author	201

25% OFF COUPON

For 25% off your first order, sign up to my mailing list!

https://mikalaneshop.com/

1

GARNET

WANTED: NICE GUY TO MARRY. I HAVE 30 DAYS TO GET MARRIED OR I LOSE FIVE MILLION DOLLARS. Me: 25, tall, big booty, long hair, regular job that pays ok. You: smart, funny, in good shape, nice guy with manners. Non-smokers only. Please respond with info about yourself and a photo. Thanks!

How lame was I, placing a Craigslist ad for a husband? But how the hell else was I going to find a husband in order to claim five million dollars in—oh, by the way—thirty freaking days?

I had weighed all the options. I really had.

First, I'd thought about walking up to some random guy on the street and proposing marriage. Yeah, like that would work. He'd run off so fast, he'd leave skid marks.

So, I played with the idea of using one of those online

dating sites. But those suckers cost money, and besides, I'd have to write a bunch of crap about myself and post a picture, and I wasn't ready for the world to know I might be inheriting a sizeable estate. At least not off the bat.

Last, I considered asking one of the guys who frequented the bar where I worked to marry me, but to be honest, I didn't want to *date* any of those dudes, much less marry one. Scratch that.

So I was left with the good old standby for reaching the masses in the internet age, Craigslist. Hell, I'd used that site to find my crappy apartment and crappy job. Why couldn't I use it to find a crappy husband?

Kidding about the crappy husband piece.

I read my ad one last time and pressed *submit*. Honestly, what more was there to say than what I'd included? I didn't want romantic walks on the beach or conversations that carried into the night. I wasn't dying for the joys of motherhood (although I wasn't opposed to it), or for someone who'd make love to me for hours (I wasn't opposed to it either, but still). And, I didn't care if the guy had money or not. If all went according to plan, *I'd* have plenty when all was said and done.

What did I have to lose? All replies to my post would go to an anonymous mailbox, thanks to the magic that was Craigslist. I'd read through a few replies, weed out the crazies, meet a couple dudes, and make my selection.

Simple, right?

I'd have my answer shortly.

While I let the internet work its magic, I hopped in the

shower to get ready for my shift at the Drive By Saloon. Corny name, I know, but it was my home away from home, and I made enough there to cover the rent on my little apartment and make the minimum payment on my student loans—for a degree I never finished, I might add. Which meant I'd be paying those loans for damn near the rest of my life at the rate I was going.

You know how people gripe about it being hard "to get ahead?" Well, I'm the poster child for that shit.

I stepped out of the shower into my freezing, unheated bathroom. San Francisco doesn't get particularly cold in the winter, thank god, but the lousy heat in the old buildings meant you were never really warm enough without a few space heaters overloading the circuits. But that's what cheap rent got you. I bundled up in my fluffy robe and began working on my hair when I heard a string of beeps coming from my laptop. The kind that notify you when an email comes in.

I heard a few more.

Then I heard a bunch.

Beep, beep, beep, beep...

And suddenly, my little laptop wouldn't shut up.

What the hell?

I ran over to it, hoping against hope that it wasn't dying just yet. It *was* on its last legs—I mean, I'd had it since college (that degree I never finished, remember?)—and I was in no position at the moment to buy a new one. And I needed it for my husband hunt.

Please don't fail me now.

It flickered to life when I opened it, and I saw my email downloads go from fifty, to a hundred, to two hundred...

Holy shit, was there a limit on how many emails you could get at once? I think I was about to find out.

The messages, which kept scrolling by as they downloaded too fast to read, numbered upward of three hundred in just minutes. They all started with *you have received a reply to your Craigslist post...*

So I opened a couple.

Hey baby, let's meet up. I could use a rich wife.

I've wanted to get married for years. Hit me up.

I'm not in it for the money, I swear.

You sound like a nice lady. Let's get married. I promise I won't bother you. My dark days are behind me now.

Good grief. Is this what Craigslist got you these days? I didn't expect Prince Charming, but I wasn't expecting abject bottom-dwellers, either. The emails continued to scroll by, finally slowing as they approached a count of four hundred.

Then came the dick pics.

Some were big, some small, some hard, some soft. Some had shaved pubes, and others looked like they were wearing little hair sweaters.

This couldn't really be how people met these days, could it?

I closed my laptop in a panic. If this was all I had to choose from, I was never going to get that damn money.

MIKA LANE

2

NATHANIEL "NAT"

I WAS FUCKING EXHAUSTED, HAVING CAUGHT A SIX A.M. flight from New York to make a meeting back in San Francisco the same morning with a new client.

Why was I doing this to myself? It's not like I got paid for the extra work at the accounting firm that took such advantage of me.

The irony. I dealt with multi-million dollar clients, but had to beg for a little raise.

Of course, it didn't help that I'd been out 'til two in the morning the night before with a hottie from the New York office. I know you're not supposed to dip your pen in the company inkwell, but I figured shit, she was three thousand miles away and we worked on different teams... what was the harm? Besides, I hadn't fucked her. But she did give me the blowie of a lifetime.

I'd had just enough time before my meeting to run out for a third cup of coffee. At all costs, I avoided the free slop from the company lunchroom. I left that for truly dire emergencies, and I wasn't that bad off yet.

On my way out, I stuck my head into my boss's office. She had a *real* office I supposed because she was a real, licensed accountant. It had windows and a table in the corner where she could hold small meetings, and a door that closed, all indications that within the office hierarchy, she was closer to the top than most of us. My office, on the other hand, was an interior one that was more like a converted broom closet. But, hey, it was a step up from the cube I used to camp out in.

"Sandra, you want a coffee? I'm running out," I asked.

She looked up from the papers she was poring over. Damn, she looked more tired than I did.

"No thanks, Nat. I'll just grab some from the break room."

Yuck. Suit yourself.

As I was exiting the building, my cell rang. It was Rick Jones, one of the guys from the Dolphin Club, a bunch of crazies I swam with every so often in the freezing water of the San Francisco Bay.

"Hey, buddy," I answered.

"Nat. How are things?" Jonesy asked.

"Man, I'm exhausted. Just got back from New York in time for an eleven a.m. meeting with a big client."

"They're working you hard."

"I know, right? I'm just hoping it pays off when they add new partners to their roster at the end of the year."

"Good luck with that. The hours I worked to become a

partner at the firm here just about killed me. But I have to say, it was worth it."

Of course it was worth it for him. Jonesy was with one of the biggest law firms in San Francisco, and since he'd made partner, he'd bought a sweet house in Pacific Heights and a hot little Porsche. He was also reportedly dating some former model from Maxim.

Asshole.

"So, Nat, I'm calling you for a reason," he continued. "I may have a client for you, who needs a good accountant. I'm not at liberty to tell you much. But I'd like to pass your info on to this woman so she's set up with you, if and when she needs someone."

"Thanks man, I appreciate the referral. And if this is a good client, it'll help me shine in my boss's eyes, too," I said.

If there was one way to climb the ranks of my firm, it was bringing in clients. Maybe I'd end up in an office with a window sooner than I thought.

NOT THREE HOURS LATER, I was looking for some bar in the South of Market District called the Drive By Saloon. Normally, we accountants held meetings in offices and conference rooms, but if a potential client wanted to meet at a drinking establishment, who was I to argue? I was only sorry it was too early in the day to have a beer. It probably would have been a free one. And until I made partner, I consumed all the free beer I could get my hands on. I hadn't "made it" yet, like Jonesy had. But I was working on it.

I pulled open a heavy wooden door that was otherwise pretty nondescript, and entered a room so dark I had to wait for my eyes to adjust. When they did, I found myself in an old-time establishment, the kind you didn't see much of in San Francisco. The setup was the standard bar extending the length of the room on one side, with booths and benches running along the other. Ceiling fans swung lazily from above, most likely left from the days when you could smoke indoors. In fact, the place still smelled smoky, even though it had been decades since anyone probably had lit up in there.

I grabbed a booth after nodding at a couple of guys settled in at the bar, who looked like regulars. Actually, they looked like they lived in the damn place.

"What can I get you, sir?" a voice called from behind the bar.

"I'm here to see Garnet Foster," I said to the man, who I guessed bussed tables and did other dirty work, judging by the greasy handprints on his white apron.

"Garnet!" he hollered, bringing some life to the place.

I ordered a ginger ale while I waited, and settled into a booth. Finally, a figure emerged from the back.

Whoa. Jonesy hadn't told me everything.

A tall, curvy woman approached, wearing those high-heeled boots all the chicks were wearing, with what I think they also called *skinny jeans*. It was a hot-as-hell look, making even the shortest girls look like they had legs that stretched for miles.

"I'm Garnet," she said, extending her hand.

I stood to greet her.

"Nat. Nat Levinson. Good to meet you."

As soon as she slipped into the booth opposite me, she waved at the small guy cleaning up behind the bar.

"How 'bout a couple Stellas?" she called.

Looked like I was going to get my beer, after all. The day was definitely looking up. Now if I could keep from falling asleep in this woman's face, I'd be in really good shape.

"Garnet, your attorney, Rick Jones, suggested you might be needing some accounting and other financial services. I take it this is your bar?"

Her eyes grew wide. "Oh, god no. I don't own this dump." She threw her head back and released a deep, sexy laugh. My dick twitched a little, which surprised the hell out of me considering the hummer I'd gotten just hours earlier.

"Well, it's a cool place," I said, waving with my beer bottle. "I love bars like this. But if this isn't yours, what is the source of your assets?"

She looked confused for a second, and it occurred to me that maybe Jonesy sent me to her by mistake. I usually worked with people and companies with a lot of money, and who were pretty savvy about using it to get even more—knowledge that I hoped would rub off on me, over time.

"What do you mean?" she asked politely.

Was I wasting my time here? Perhaps, but she *was* hot, and there was no reason to be an ass to her.

"Sorry Garnet. People hire a firm like mine when they need help managing large sums of money. That's why I thought maybe you owned the bar. They typically take in a lot of cash."

She brightened and nodded. "Right. Well, I can tell you that they do. But I think you're right about my needing your help."

3

GARNET

THE ACCOUNTING GUY MY LAWYER HAD SENT WAS CUTE, IN a straight-laced way—but shouldn't an accountant look kind of straight-laced, anyway? If he'd come in looking like a rock star, I'd probably have sent him packing.

He sucked down his beer in record time, so I had another brought over. God, I was itching to touch that preppy, close-cropped blond hair that made him look like an Abercrombie & Fitch or Ralph Lauren model. And from what I could tell, under his suit and now-loosened tie, he looked pretty damn buff. My devious plan was to keep feeding him beers so he had to eventually run to the restroom. Then I could get a look at his butt.

Why weren't guys like *this* on Craigslist? Damn.

While he was no doubt nice to look at, I wasn't entirely sure why I was meeting with him. It seemed the lawyer who'd come to tell me about my inheritance had been premature in recommending him. If I didn't meet the pretty-much-impossible stipulation of finding a husband in the required thirty-day timeframe, I'd not get a penny of the five million. This guy seemed to know nothing about this vital detail, which was fine with me. I didn't want him or anyone else to know the details of my situation. I'd read what happened to people who suddenly came into money. I didn't want to set the sharks circling a moment earlier than I had to.

"Nat, I can't really share much with you yet, but I should know whether or not I will in the next few weeks. Certainly by the end of the month."

Yup. By the end of the month, I'd know whether I'd be stuck in bartender servitude for the remainder of my life or have the chance to realize my dreams...

"Garnet, can you point me toward the restroom, please?" he asked.

Score!

"Right back that way," I said, pointing. I needed to wrap things up, anyway. The happy hour crowd would be filtering in shortly.

But he did give me the chance to watch him walk away, a fact that was not lost on the two regulars at the bar, who laughed and shook their heads at me. I'd be getting shit from them later, for sure.

But I didn't care. He was well over six feet tall with wide shoulders I'd not appreciated until I saw him standing. And while his suit jacket covered most of the goods, I could tell there was a nice, firm butt under his suit pants. I hadn't seen anyone this nice-looking in a long time. I was clearly hanging out in the wrong places.

Don't get me wrong. I had great affection for the Drive By Saloon. It attracted locals and other old-timers who loved a bar they felt at home in. In fact, it was one of these regulars who got me in the situation I was in, looking for a husband with fewer than thirty days to spare.

Just three days earlier, a lawyer had come by the bar. He looked around pretty much the same way Nat had—clearly these guys didn't frequent dumps like this. But Rick Jones, Esquire, took me to one of the booths in the back to sit down and talk about one of the bar's regulars.

"Garnet, I'm here to tell you your customer, Bill Cordy, recently passed away."

What? Bill Cordy? Who the hell was that?

Puzzled, I shook my head. "I'm sorry but I don't know a Bill Cordy."

The attorney nodded, as if he'd anticipated my reaction. "I thought as much. Apparently, he was a regular here for a long time. His will mentioned that you and the others called him 'Grandpa.'"

Holy shit, now I knew who he was talking about! Grandpa. And Grandpa was gone. Now I felt badly for not knowing his real name, but the truth was, he would spend hours sipping on the same beer, staring at the ass of any female behind the bar. And that female was usually me.

To be honest, I thought he was a creepy perv who, by

the way, never tipped. Not that I wanted to think ill of the dead.

"Wow. Okay, I know exactly who you are talking about. How'd he die?"

And more importantly, why did a lawyer come to tell me this?

But first things first.

He flipped through some papers as if the question hadn't crossed his mind. "Looks like he died in his sleep. Old age, that sort of thing." He shrugged. "Guess that's how we'd all like to go."

I didn't spend much time thinking about how I wanted to go. I was only twenty-five years old. But I still wasn't sure how any of this concerned me.

"Thanks for letting me know. I'll be sure to share it with the rest of the staff as well as some of the other regulars." I glanced at the wall clock as the happy hour crowd started to trickle in. Heaven forbid they miss out on their dollar beers. I started to get up from the booth.

"Garnet, that's not all I came to talk about," he said with his hand up in the *wait a minute* position.

I lowered myself back into the booth. I wish he'd get on with whatever he needed. I was sorry Grandpa was gone, but I didn't really even know the guy.

"Bill Cordy, the man you called Grandpa, left you his estate."

Now *that* made me laugh. Loudly

"I guess that comes as a surprise to you?" the lawyer asked.

Um, yeah.

"Grandpa—I mean Bill Cordy—had an estate? And he left it to me? Don't tell me. I get to take his cats or something?" Good grief, not only did the guy never tip me, now I had to take care of his damn cats?

He laughed. "Sounds like you don't like cats. And lucky for you, he didn't have any. But what he did leave you, Garnet, was an estate worth five million dollars."

I'd been looking over his shoulder at my co-bartender who was hustling drinks for the happy hour cheapies and giving me dirty looks from across the room.

"Be right there!" I called to him.

Wait. What?

"Did you just say something about five million dollars?"

"He had an estate worth five million dollars, and it's been left to you. All of it." He looked like he delivered news like this all the time. Maybe he did. But not to people like me.

I placed my hands on the scruffy booth table. I didn't usually like to touch them, coated as they were with years of carvings, burn marks, and water stains, but I needed to keep my balance.

I opened my mouth to speak. "Wha…how…why…?" The blood had rushed to my head even though I was seated. I didn't know that could even happen.

"Um, are you okay, Garnet?" the lawyer asked.

He clearly didn't see a reaction like mine often. And I didn't know if I was okay.

"Excuse me for a moment. I'll be right back," I said and ran for the ladies' room, where I heaved over the toilet for a minute. I put a cool paper towel on the back of my neck and returned to the booth where the lawyer waited. I wanted to hear all about this dumb joke someone was clearly playing on me.

I took my seat. "This really isn't funny. In fact, it's kind of mean."

He nodded kindly. "I understand. But I can assure you this is real. I have a copy of Mr. Cordy's will right here for you. I can also see you're needing to get to work though, so I want to make this fast. There is one stipulation to your receiving the estate." His eyebrows rose like he was waiting for me to hang on his every word.

Wow. He wasn't giving up the joke.

It *was* a joke, right?

"Okay, Mr. Jones," I said, feeling ballsy. If he wanted to fuck with me, I could fuck with him right back. "Give me your worst."

That got a smile out of him.

"The stipulation—Mr. Cordy seemed to feel strongly about it—is that you have thirty days to get married."

Oh. That's all? Just a little thing like getting married.

He didn't wait for me to respond. "Do you have a boyfriend? Someone you were already planning to marry, anyway?"

He pushed my copy of the will in front of me. I was no expert but it looked pretty damn authentic.

Shit.

I shook my head slowly. I wished he had never come into the bar and bothered me with this nonsense. My life would have been perfectly fine without it. I'd woken up that morning with nothing, and if I went to bed that night with nothing, I'd be no better or worse off.

Instead, my simple existence had just flown out the window.

NAT RETURNED to the table to find me deep in thought. So deep in fact, that he had to tap my shoulder.

"Garnet? You okay?" he asked.

I snapped back to reality. "Oh. Yeah. Sorry."

The lawyer had connected me with this guy in case I got the goods. Which was silly because my chances of that, given Grandpa's stipulation, were slim to none.

"I'm fine, Nat. Thank you for asking." I stood and extended my hand.

He looked around, as if hoping for privacy, and lowered his voice. "I don't usually do this…I mean, ask clients out…but since you're not a client and may never be, would you like to go out? Get coffee, a drink, even dinner?"

Shit. Maybe meeting Grandpa's demand was not going to be as impossible as I'd thought.

MIKA LANE

4

LINCOLN "LINC"

My brother sauntered into our shared office wearing a shit-eating grin, as if he were the luckiest guy in the world. I suppose that, at that moment in time, he probably was.

"What, Jack?" I asked, all accusation and suspicion.

"Whaddya mean, what?" he asked, shrugging dramatically. He leaned back in his chair, hands behind his head, kicking his Nikes up on the desk. What a dick.

"Dude. I know you're fucking around with Monica," I said.

He whipped around to face me. "So? So what, Linc? We don't all want to live like monks, you know. Some of us like to express our sexual selves."

I rolled my eyes. "*Sexual selves?* Where did you get that? Have you been watching Oprah again?" He watched daytime TV with the female gym employees when they were on break. Said it made him look like a 'sensitive guy.'

He rolled his eyes and turned back to his computer. "Whatever."

That about summed it up. Jack had always been the popular one with the never-ending stream of women and girlfriends, and I was the shy, quiet one who could barely look at a female, never mind speak to one. High school might have been many years behind us, but things weren't really all that different.

"Jack, I know I've said this before, but messing around with employees will not end well. It might be fun in the moment, but please, just date the members or something." I waved my hand at the office window that overlooked our exercise room. "There are tons of beautiful women out there. Lay off the employees."

He shrugged. "I know you're right, Linc. It's just that when they throw themselves at me, it's so hard to say no. Especially that one with the huge…"

"Okay, Jack! I'm done here. I'm heading next door for a beer before going home. I've had a long day."

He smiled. I knew what he was going to throw at me.

"Right, little bro. You started the day with your touchy-feely yoga class before the sun was even up. No wonder you're tired." Suddenly, his eyes widened. "Hey… how come I never thought of that? Yoga…hot women in tight clothing. Shit. Why've you been holding out on me? I'm joining tomorrow."

"Later, Jack," I said, letting the office door slam behind me for emphasis.

"Save me a seat at the bar," he called.

I pushed open the door to the dive bar around the corner from our gym, where I'd been only a couple times before. Jack and I worked such long hours, we rarely had downtime to just sit and have a beer. The Drive By was kind of a smelly dump, but the beer was cold and cheap, and most times, that was all I needed. I settled onto a barstool and ordered myself a Michelob Ultra. Tasted like crap, but at least it was low in carbs.

The bar was fairly crowded, with old dudes who looked like regulars clustered down at one end and yuppies slumming it at the other. I kept to myself, as usual, while I waited on my brother.

I heard a voice in my ear.

"Don't worry, you'll get to use that pretty mouth on me later."

WHAT? I whipped around to find the dude who was talking to me like that. But I was alone. No one was even next to me. I turned back to my beer.

"Baby, I can't wait to see you gag on me," the voice said.

Shit. Okay, I was pretty sure that wasn't intended for me. But who *was* it intended for?

I looked around again, wondering what bag of dicks was trying to work it. It seemed I was the only one who'd heard, until I caught sight of a pretty young woman whose face was covered in fear. She was a couple barstools over, sitting with the dirty-mouthed asshole. Her upper arm was in his tight grip, indented by the pressure from his fingers. He looked pleased with his clueless seduction skills and oblivious to her desire to escape. Any idiot could see she was not enjoying herself. Except him, apparently.

"C'mon now," the guy continued smoothly. "I know where you live. So don't act like you're too good for me." His cheesy smile suggested he did that sort of thing all the time.

The woman tried to pull away, her dark curls getting caught in his grip.

"Could you please let go of me?" she asked, looking around nervously.

He released her. "Yeah. No problem. Let's get going."

Standing, he threw some money on the bar, then grabbed her hand and pulled her to her feet. That's when she caught my eye.

That was all I needed.

"Excuse me," I said to the two of them.

The guy looked me up and down. I might be a quiet guy, but I was a fucking fit one.

He was not deterred. "Bro, get out of our way." He attempted to push past me, dragging the stumbling woman.

I placed a hand on his shoulder. "It doesn't look like the lady here is either having a good time, or wanting to go anywhere with you." I turned to her for a reaction.

She quickly shook her head and looked from him to me and back. "I...I don't want to go anywhere with you. Please leave me alone."

I turned to the guy. "Did you hear what she said? You

need to leave her alone. Or do you need me to *help* you leave her alone?" I pulled myself up to full height, a good head taller than him.

When he got a load of the disparity in our sizes, his face blanched and he dropped the woman's hand. She stepped back and partly behind me. But the guy's mouth wasn't backing down. "Fuck you, dude. Why don't you mind your fucking business?" he spat in my face.

He was dumber than I'd thought. "If it's not clear that it's time for you to leave, I will be happy to help you out the door," I said calmly.

"Fuck off," he said to me, turning to the woman. "And you, you little c—," but he didn't get to finish.

I grabbed him by the collar, dragged him through the bar, and tossed him out the door just as my brother was coming in. I pulled it closed once Jack was inside, leaving the creep out on the sidewalk on his ass.

"Hey, I got us a couple seats," I said, nodding toward the bar.

"All right then," Jack said, following me with a big smile.

5

GARNET

THAT HAD GONE WELL—*NOT*. I'D WEEDED THROUGH ALL those damn Craigslist emails, looked at an untold number of penis photographs, and chose the one guy I thought was not a complete psycho. There had to be one good one in there, right? Wrong. He might have been the best of the worst, but I quickly learned that wasn't saying a hell of a lot.

And now I was face to face with the Adonis of a guy who'd thrown my creepy Craigslist date out the door and onto his ass. And if that weren't embarrassing enough, another fellow joined him who could have been his twin. Good grief, there were two of them?

"Hey, are you okay? That guy was a real asshole."

He was freaking gorgeous with his scruff of facial hair and slightly unkempt ponytail.

But even though the creep was gone, I was still shaken. I could play it cool, though. I flipped my hair back in my best *no big deal* fashion. Adonis didn't look fooled.

"Um, yeah, I'm fine." I forced a small smile. "Thank you. I really appreciate it. Are you sitting here?" I gestured to an empty seat at the bar. His twin, or whatever he was, had already made himself at home on his other side.

"Yes. But I want to make sure you're okay." The sensitivity in his eyes contrasted with his muscular bulk. It was like seeing a unicorn.

"I'm fine, thanks to you. Let me get you a beer." I waved over my coworker, who was chatting it up with the regulars at the end of the bar. God, I hoped none of them had witnessed my humiliation. No more meeting potential dates at my place of employment. I'd thought it would be safe, and it probably was, but my pathetic attempts to meet a guy needed to remain private.

"Really, you don't need to."

"Don't worry. I work here so I get them for free. Even when I'm off duty."

He laughed, lightening the moment. I grabbed the stool next to him. Maybe the night wouldn't be a complete bust, after all.

He studied me. "I thought you looked familiar." He sipped his Mic Ultra.

Funny he recognized me, yet I didn't remember ever having seen him. It was doubtful I could forget a man like that, but maybe he'd come in when we were busy.

"Do you come here regularly? I'm surprised we haven't met." I extended my hand. "I'm Garnet."

"Garnet, nice to meet you. I'm Linc. And this is my brother, Jack."

Dayum.

"Ha! I thought you guys were related! Twins?"

"No. But a lot of people ask us that. My brother here is the older one." He slapped Jack on the shoulder. "I still have my youth," Linc said with a crooked grin.

Jack pushed his brother's hand off his shoulder like it was an annoying fly. "Yeah, but I got the good looks."

Their rap was cute.

"So, Garnet, what was that creep doing in here?"

Ugh. He had to ask that. Of course. It was inevitable.

I could fabricate an answer. Like he was an abusive ex-husband, or an actor practicing lines for an upcoming play.

But I couldn't lie to save my life. "He was an online date."

He grimaced. "Ouch. Damn. Talk about the dark side of internet dating."

"Yup. Live and learn. I'll never do that again."

I'd probably also never have five million dollars, but it wasn't for lack of trying.

"You seem like a nice woman. You need to be careful." He took a sip of his beer. "I have to say, I don't understand why you tried online dating to begin with."

"Why?" I asked. If he was going to be all judgey, he could go to hell.

"Well, because look at you. I mean, you must have guys pounding your door down." He was completely serious.

Now *that* was funny.

"Yeah, well. The same could be said of you."

"What? Me?" he asked.

"Yeah. Why don't you have a girlfriend?"

Ooh. Did I just say that? But I was already humiliated, so why not completely ruin the evening?

He turned pink, then bright red, looking into his beer like he wanted to crawl inside it and die.

"Oh, I'm sorry. You *do* have a girlfriend. I shouldn't make assumptions."

He shook his head slowly, still not looking up. "Yeah, no, I don't have a girlfriend." He glanced over at his brother, who was chatting up the cute girl sitting on his other side. Then he turned to me.

"Why'd you put yourself in a situation like that, where you ended up with someone who could have hurt you?"

Well, shit. I could tell him the whole Grandpa story, but that was so un-freaking-believable I wobbled back and forth between accepting it and thinking I'd imagined the whole thing.

"Um, you know. Just thought it might be nice to meet someone. So I put an ad on Craigslist."

"Craigslist? Why not a real dating site, like Match.com or something?"

"I have my reasons. Anyway, you live around here?" Time to change the subject from my love life.

"Not far. My brother and I own the gym around the corner," he said.

"No way! I know that place. So it's yours? Yours and Jack's? It's sort of new, right?"

He smiled with pride. "Yeah, coming up on a year. And what a year it's been."

"Really?" I asked.

My coworker Tom set two fresh beers in front of us. "It's been pretty up and down. We'll be busy, signing up members, and then things will slow. You know, every business has its ups and downs. Hey, you should join my bootcamp exercise class. Not that you need it. It's just a lot of fun."

"Oh, really? Well, I wouldn't mind more exercise. But, not sure I have time." Though I should probably find a way to make time, if for no other reason than to watch him flex what looked like some very nice muscles under the jeans and pullover he was wearing.

"Seriously. I'll give you a discount."

I'd have to be an idiot to say no to that.

"Thank you. I'll let you know. That's so cool you have a business with your brother."

"It is nice. We're tight. Really stick together."

Jack appeared, tapping Linc on the shoulder.

"We got an early morning, bro," Jack said.

Linc glanced at his watch. "Ugh. No rest for the weary. The gym opens at six a.m. So guess who has to be there?"

"Well, it was nice meeting you both," I said. "And thank you again for your help."

On impulse, I threw my arms around him to emphasize my appreciation. I had to force myself to let go. And he smelled damn good.

"Yeah, Garnet. Good meeting you, too. Please come by the gym. Here's my business card."

After they left, I sat at the bar a bit longer. No sense rushing home to my crummy apartment when I could hang out in a crummy bar.

When I did get home, I called my best friend, Matty.

"Bitch!" he screamed into the phone. "Why'd you take so long to call me? Was tonight's date the one? 'Cause I know you're gonna get that five million so you can take me on a big-ass vacation. Preferably someplace with men wearing little Speedos…a cruise would be quite nice…"

"God, Matty. Put your dick back in your pants, would you?" I plopped down on the overstuffed chair I'd picked up at a garage sale. It was coming apart at a couple seams, but I was attached to the sorry little thing.

I continued. "The guy was a psycho." Saying those words out loud was sad. Just freaking sad. "I'm kind of disappointed. He seemed so nice over email."

"Look, I told you not to use Craigslist. And take it from me, 'cause us queens meet our booty calls there all the time—the internet is not where you find a husband."

"I know that now, Matty. You were right. But I did meet someone else. Sort of."

"Get out. You're putting it out there, girl. I know you'll find someone. You'll get that money, and you'll finally get laid."

Ouch. It *had* been awhile. Only I didn't need the biggest slut in town to remind me of it.

"So there was this big guy who saw my date harassing me. He grabbed him by the collar and threw him out the door."

He shrieked. He loved tough guys and drama. Two in one were almost too much for him to bear.

"What did he look like? What was his name? And did he have a job?" Because Matty was not too particular, he ended up with a lot of dates with questionable backgrounds and unstable employment. If they had any employment at all. The last guy he'd dated had been in prison for selling drugs.

"Well," I said, smiling. "He was really tall. I mean I had to look up at him."

That didn't happen often when you were my height of five foot ten.

"Super broad shoulders, really muscular from what I could tell. Messy little ponytail, some beard scruff, and these pretty blue eyes with the longest lashes. How come guys get the good lashes?"

"Damn, Gar. You did all right. Think you'll see him again?" Matty asked.

I was counting on it.

"He owns the gym around the corner from Drive By Saloon. He invited me to join his bootcamp class."

"Oh. My. God. A dumb jock. You hit booty jackpot."

"Well, I don't know that he's a dumb jock—"

"Gar, gotta run. I have a call coming in. Love you!"

And he was gone.

It was okay, though. That was how we operated. He had a date, or booty call, or something lined up, and I never got in the way.

He never got in my way, either. That was why we were best friends.

6

BALDWIN "WIN"

THINGS HADN'T CHANGED MUCH SINCE OLD MAN CORDY had kicked the bucket. And I was hoping everything would stay that way.

His lawyer had come by a couple days after I found him dead in the house, when the cops had come and the coroner had taken him away. I wasn't sure what to do after that, so I just kept working, keeping up the house and property, and minding my own business in the apartment over the garage.

The lawyer told me they'd be figuring out what was to happen with Cordy's estate in the next few days, and to just hang tight. I was going to miss him. The old man had been more of a father to me than my own father.

I was busy trimming some hedges and enjoying the fresh smell of the incoming San Francisco Bay tide when I saw a woman on the property. I'd known it was just a matter of time before someone from Cordy's family came sniffing around to see if there was anything they could get now that he was six feet under. Damn vultures. I had to say, though, this particular one was quite the looker. Crazy long hair and some tight-ass jeans. Shit.

"Yo," I hollered.

She looked around, having heard me, but unable to figure out where my voice had come from.

"Hello?" she called.

"Over here." If she'd come to cash in on Cordy's death, I was going to make her walk over to me and not the other way around.

"Oh, hi," she said, waving.

"Can I help you, miss?"

Her mouth opened, and it looked like she was trying to figure out how to explain herself. I'd seen it before. It was what liars did.

"I...um...I was looking into, um, checking out the house." She nodded like she needed to convince herself more than me. "I, um, heard it might be for lease. It's a pretty awesome place. Do you work here?"

No, I hang out and trim bushes for a good time.

"Yes. I am the groundskeeper, property manager, whatever you want to call it."

"Oh. Did you know Gran—I mean, Bill Cordy?"

"Of course. This was his place, until..." God, I was going to miss the son of a bitch.

She looked around, taking in the view of the sailboats in the distance. Shit, I hoped I wouldn't have to leave the property. It was one of the few residences on the water in Belvedere, a tiny community just outside San Francisco. Cordy's huge stone house sat on a spit of land that extended into the Bay with perfect views of downtown San Francisco on the other side of the water. It was magical and a far cry from what I'd grown up with.

"Yes, I heard he passed." She looked at me. "Had you worked for him for long?"

I pulled off my gardening gloves and pushed back my hair. My own dad had kicked me out when I'd gotten busted for pot. Cordy had offered me the little apartment above his garage, and in exchange, I was to do some work around his house. That was twelve years ago.

And twelve years since I'd heard from my asshole father.

So, yeah, I had a bit of an attitude about someone snooping around the property. Even if they did claim to be interested in leasing it.

And even if they were as good-looking as the woman who stood before me just then.

And don't you know, she had the nicest eyes I'd seen in a long time, and her crooked little smile gave me a tic like a teenage boy.

But still…

Oh, what the hell. "Yeah, I've worked here for quite awhile. I suppose you'd like to see the house?" I offered.

She clasped her hands. "Really? I'd love to, if that's okay. Are you sure?"

"Yup. Cordy's gone. It's just me on the property now." I

shot her a dirty look as we headed up to the house. "For the time being, anyway."

"Right. Will you just stay on here?"

"I'm hoping so. But it all depends on what happens with the estate."

She tilted her head. "Really? What have you heard?"

I shrugged. "Nothing really. A lawyer came around a few days ago and told me he'd get back to me."

I took the keys off my belt and let us into the kitchen.

"I hate that feeling of being unsettled. I mean, I *would* hate it. If I were in your shoes."

She was so sincere.

And cute as hell, no doubt about it. But something about her seemed the tiniest bit nervous. Like she wasn't being completely honest with me. I had a good sense about people that way.

"What's your name?" I asked her.

"Garnet. Garnet Foster." She extended her hand.

"You can call me Win. Where'd you get a name like Garnet, anyway?"

"It's my birthstone, so my parents decided to name me after it." She shook her head, her long waves bouncing around. "I like having an unusual name. What about Win? Where'd you get that name?"

"Win is short for Baldwin. Baldwin Ronan," I told her.

She looked around the kitchen where I'd shared so many meals with Cordy. Damn, was that a lump building in my throat? I swallowed hard, not wanting to share my grief with a person I didn't know.

But I guess I didn't hide it well enough. She put a hand on my arm.

"If this isn't a good time, I can come back," she offered.

Get it together, dude. I cleared my throat.

"No, you're here now. Let's get you a look at the place." I led her through the dining room into the foyer, a majestic space with a wide staircase leading to the upper floors. That was where her mouth dropped open.

"Oh my God, I've never in all my life seen anything like this." Wide eyed, she made a complete circle to take it all in, giving me the opportunity to check out her curvy ass.

"Yup. It's pretty awesome. C'mon, let's go upstairs."

I had her peek into each of the four bedrooms on the second floor, all with their own bathrooms, and the additional ones on the top floor. I looked out one of the windows toward the Bay and watched a sailboat tilting in the wind.

She clasped her hands together. "Thank you, Win, for showing me around. The place is truly amazing."

"How'd you know about it, anyway? Cordy passed only last week," I asked.

She opened her mouth but nothing came out, and she turned several shades of pink. Yup, just as I suspected. "I, um, found out from the lawyer. Probably the same one who spoke to you. We were…connected by a mutual acquaintance." She started moving toward the door.

I thought fast—I didn't want to let her go until I learned more about her and her interest in Cordy's house.

I checked my watch, and we descended the stairs back to the foyer.

"So Garnet, if you don't have to run, I'd be happy to show you the grounds. My workday is winding down."

She slowed down, clearly intrigued by the offer. "Oh! I'd like that, thanks."

I led her outside, past the rose garden to the redwood grove that grew right up to the cliffs overlooking the water.

"Let's have a seat," I offered, pointing to a couple Adirondack chairs.

"It's breathtaking," she said, taking it all in. She was right.

"So, Garnet Foster, where do you live now? How are you gonna live in a big house like this all by yourself?"

She swallowed hard. I figured she was thinking through the next lie she wanted to lay on me.

"Oh, well, I could always get a roommate, you know." She glanced back at the house. "I'm not sure it's for me, though, to be honest. I don't know if I could afford a place like that."

"What kind of work do you do?" I asked her.

"I'm a bartender. The Drive By Saloon. Ever been there?" she asked.

I'd heard Cordy talk about hanging out there. Maybe that was how she found out about the house? I had figured she was just nosing around, and it looked like I'd been right. A bartender couldn't rent a mansion in Belvedere. Did she think I was a freaking idiot?

"I've never been there, but I remember hearing Cordy talk about it. In fact, I might even have heard him talk about you." Now that I thought about it, I wondered if this was the bartender he'd taken a liking to.

Her eyes opened wide. "Really? He talked about me?"

"I remember him talking about someone there who he liked."

She tilted her head toward me. "You're kidding. He barely ever spoke to me. I didn't think he even knew that much about me."

"He seemed fond of you. Said you were a hard-working young lady who was very nice. Maybe he also had a bit of a crush on you."

She threw her head back and laughed. "I can believe that. He tended to stare a lot."

I still wasn't sure why she was snooping around the property, but now that I knew she had a connection to Cordy, it was coming together. I found myself not wanting her to leave, and not only because I wanted to know what she was up to.

"Hey, there are some beers up at the house. Would you like one?"

7

GARNET

Oh. My. God. Cordy's house was insane. I never would have guessed, not in a million years, that he lived like this. He had always looked borderline homeless.

Mom had always said, "Don't judge a book by its cover."

Lesson learned.

And to make things a bit more interesting, his groundskeeper was off-the-charts hot. The guy's bright blue eyes popped against his tan, lined face. From his rugged appearance, I guessed he must have spent a great deal of his life working outdoors. He was so good looking in fact, that I had trouble keeping my story straight about Cordy and why I was there at the house. And while I eventually won him over, he had clearly not been happy when he first found me checking out the property.

In fact, I thought initially he was going to kick me out for trespassing. He'd been kind of aggro, with the way he confronted me. But I guess he changed his mind. Of course, it helped that I was wearing my tightest blue jeans and some high-heeled boots that gave a nice little lift to my butt.

I followed him from the redwood grove where we'd been talking, back up to the house to take him up on the beer he'd offered. It didn't seem likely I'd ever get to live in Cordy's incredible house, but it sure would be fun to dream about it. Thirty days were going by freakishly fast, and I wasn't any closer to having a husband than I'd been the day the lawyer had come to see me at the saloon.

But that hadn't stopped me from fantasizing about what I'd do if I *did* get five million dollars. First, getting my student loan debt off my back would be a dream come true. Not a week went by when I didn't wake up in the middle of the night from a nightmare about all that I owed and how unlikely it was I could ever pay it off. But even better would be the opportunity to do something, even if it were a small effort, to help others. I'd begin with the homeless people in my neighborhood. I had no illusions that I could solve San Francisco's homeless problem, but I could start in my own backyard.

Oh, why was I torturing myself? It was beyond ridiculous.

"Thank you," I said, taking a beer from Win. I grabbed a stool at the spotless kitchen counter, and he sat right next to me. He smelled like he'd been gardening—a sexy scent of flowers, fresh dirt, and a bit of sweat.

I'd better watch it, having a beer with a man like him.

"Cheers, Garnet. It's nice to meet you, whether or not you end up leasing the place."

I could swear there was some sort of smirk on his face. I know what he was thinking—how could a girl like me, who tends bar at the down and out Drive By Saloon, possibly afford a place like this one?

Well, his initial assumption was right. He just didn't know the whole story, and I wasn't about to tell him. One thing I did know, however, was that if I did end up in that house, and he was difficult about it, I wouldn't be keeping him around. That was for sure.

Even though I was sitting so close to him now I could feel my heart pounding in my fingers and toes. Damn.

"How long did you say you'd been working here?" I asked him.

He took a sip of his beer and nodded. "Over ten years. I live in the little apartment over the garage. It's a great set up."

"Were you close with Cordy?"

He opened his mouth, then shut it. Shit. Did I say the wrong thing again?

Without a word, he nodded slowly. "He was good to me, Cordy was. Got kicked out of the house by my own old man. Cordy took me in," he answered.

"Wow. It must be hard for you, that he's gone now. Are you in contact with your dad?"

Ugh. Stuck my foot in it again. I needed to stop asking this poor guy personal questions. He looked like he wished I'd stop, too.

He shook his head. "No. No I haven't been in touch with him. And I've heard he's pretty sick, so he probably won't be around much longer."

Damn. My heart hurt for this guy. Something about him seemed so…lonely, I think it was.

"Can you reach out to your dad? I mean, what would that be like?" I asked.

"Not sure. I'm really not sure whether I want to or not."

"I get that," I said. I really did.

"What about you?" he asked. "You close with your parents?"

"Well, I never knew my dad. Not my real dad, anyway. My mom lives in Texas with her latest boyfriend. We're not very close. She sort of couldn't be bothered by me when I was growing up. Still is that way, really."

Win turned on his stool to fully face me. "Huh. Our stories are sort of similar."

We did have family issues in common, but I could hardly think about that with his blue eyes boring into mine. God, he made good eye contact. Then I made the mistake of looking at my watch.

"Shit!" I said, jumping off the barstool. "I lost track of time. I have to work in twenty minutes. Thank you for the beer." I grabbed my purse and held my hand out.

Instead, he leaned in and kissed my cheek. In doing so, he was able to let his lips linger on me long enough to make me dizzy. I grabbed the counter for balance. And if I wasn't mistaken, I think I heard him take a whiff of my hair.

"Why don't you come by the bar sometime?" I asked him.

He just looked down at me for a moment. If I didn't hustle and get out of there, I wasn't sure I ever would.

And I had lied to him about my reasons for being there. I felt shitty about that.

"I will come by," he said, tilting his head and continuing to gaze at me. "Maybe I can take Cordy's old seat."

"Oh, that would be great." He was also welcome to stare at my ass just like Cordy did. But I didn't think he needed an invitation to do that.

By the time I crossed the Golden Gate Bridge to get back into San Francisco, and then braved the rush hour traffic across town, I was almost an hour late for my shift.

"Oh my god, Tom, I'm so sorry." I slammed my things into a cabinet behind the bar and grabbed an apron.

"Slow down, cowgirl," Tom said. "We're not that busy, and I was having fun hanging with your friend down at the end of the bar."

I followed his gaze and found Matty sipping a martini. When I caught his eye, he waved at me frantically.

"I'm out of here, if you don't mind. Have a good night," Tom said.

I immediately took stock of the folks drinking at the bar to see who needed a refill and who wanted to pay their check. After I took care of a few patrons, I worked my way down to the bar toward Matty.

"Hi!" I told him. "You never come here. What's up?"

It was true. He thought the bar was a dump. Which it was. But I think that's what people liked about it.

"I had to hear about the dead guy's house. Was it amazing? Tell me!" His eyes were wild with expectation. I couldn't let him down.

But there was no need to. Grandpa's house was that incredible. I told him every last detail, stopping when I had to serve customers.

"The house was amazing," I told him, "but you should have seen the groundskeeper."

"Oh my god, tell me," he stage-whispered.

"He was like the Marlboro Man. Only better. And he didn't smoke."

Matty laughed at that.

I continued, "I'm pretty sure he was suspicious of my coming to see the house, though."

"You little slut! I love it." He clapped his hands together happily and stepped off his stool. "Well. My work here is done. I just wanted to hear the latest in your pre-millionaire adventures."

"Shhh!" I hissed, looking around. "I don't want anyone besides you to know about this."

"Don't worry, mum's the word. I just want to know

when you're bringing me by the place. I want to see it so bad."

"Okay. I'll see if I can arrange it. But you have to be cool. You can't let on what's going on."

"I'll be good. I swear I'll be good," he assured me, and he made for the door, most likely to head out to meet that evening's date.

I wasn't sure how I could get Matty there without *really* raising Win's suspicions. But hell, what would I do if the place really did become mine some day? There'd be no hiding that. Shit, what if I ended up being Win's boss?

8

AMBROSE "BROSE"

My best buddy Win and I headed into the city to some dive bar to see a girl he'd taken a liking to.

"How'd you meet her?" I asked as he wove his pickup truck through heavy San Francisco traffic.

"Dude, it was the weirdest thing," he started. "I saw her snooping around Cordy's property. I was going to kick her the hell out, but she was just so nice. Not to mention, hot as hell."

That's my buddy Win. Always thinking with his little head.

"So, what was she doing there?" I asked.

"Well, at first, I thought for sure she was casing the place. I even offered to show her the house, just to test her and see how she reacted. But she wasn't interested in any of the valuables. Said she was looking into leasing the property. But Brose, she's a freaking bartender. She can't lease a mansion on the water."

I watched my friend shake his head. Win had a lot of street smarts, and if he felt something was off, it probably was.

"All right. So if it all seemed so fishy, why are you going to see her?" I gave him the side-eye, like I always did when I thought he was being an idiot.

He shrugged as he made an illegal left turn. Like I said, idiot.

"I...I can't put my finger on it. She's just cute. I want to know her more." He looked over at me.

"I think you'll like her, too," he added.

"Ah, okay. I know where you're going with this now. Why you wanted me to come." I looked out the window and laughed. I should have figured this out when he insisted I join him.

"I don't know, dude, don't write it off. It worked out pretty well when we both dated Esme.

"That was cool as shit. Until she moved back to France, anyway."

Win nodded, wistfulness washing over his face. He'd really loved her. Hell, I had, too.

He pulled up to the curb in a funky South of Market neighborhood and headed for a nondescript door on a building with no street-facing windows.

"Guess I know why they call this the Drive By Saloon. If you didn't know it was here, you'd never notice it," I said.

"Yeah, looks nice and dumpy. Just what the doctor ordered." Win pulled the door open with a huge grin and let me enter first. He was in his element.

IT WAS DIM INSIDE, enough so that I had to let my eyes adjust to the lack of light. When I could finally see, we headed for a long, wooden bar that must have been a hundred years old. Definitely a neighborhood place from the look of the geezer patrons and a couple yuppies in the corner enjoying cheap beer. A young guy with tattoos and thick silver earrings approached us with a bar mop in hand.

"What can I get you, gentlemen?" he asked with a smile, wiping down the spot in front of us. The old bar's wood was stained by years of patrons spilling and breaking things. Oh, the stories it could probably tell.

"Hey, man," Win said. "How 'bout a couple Buds?"

"Coming right up," the bartender said.

I turned to Win. "Dude, you know I hate Budweiser. Why do you always insist on ordering me one?"

Win rolled his eyes, waving his arm in the air to beckon the bartender back. He gestured toward me.

"My fine friend here would like one of your floofy beers."

"Blow me," I said to Win. I looked at the amused bartender, who probably thought we were a bickering couple. "I'll have a Sierra Nevada, please."

"So Brosey," Win said to me. "What's up with the restaurant?"

I took a long draw on my beer. Damn, that was tasty. "It's going good, I think. The head chef really seems to like my work. He's giving me more to do and even asked my opinion about a couple new dishes he's working on."

"Shit, bro! That's awesome." He slapped me on the back.

Just then, the bar's front door blew open, letting in a flash of sunlight. It was gone just as quickly, reverting to its sleepy duskiness.

But it didn't close too fast for me to spot the gorgeous woman who walked in. I immediately felt a little jolt in my pants, and I hoped she'd come sit by me.

She was tall with wild long hair, dressed kind of tomboyish with a plain white T-shirt and Adidas, which was quite the contrast with her curvy-as-shit figure. She walked straight toward Win and me, her tits jiggling lightly in spite of the lacy bra visible through her shirt, her nice round hips moving side to side just so. She didn't have to try to be sexy, like some girls did, which really just killed me.

"Win!" she said as if she'd found a long-lost friend. How well did he know her? And how could I get to know her?

She threw an arm around him in a half-hug.

"I was hoping you'd come by the bar." She turned to me. "Who's your friend here?"

Holy shit. *This* was Garnet? Now I understood why we drove across town in such shitty traffic.

"Garnet, I'd like you to meet my friend, Brose, chef extraordinaire."

I popped off my seat and took Garnet's hand. And then, because I couldn't help myself, in a cheesy move I pulled it to my lips for a kiss. God, her skin smelled good. She dropped her head back and released a laugh that washed over me like some kind of damn music.

Shit. I hated it when this happened.

Win had known I'd like her, probably the moment he laid eyes on her trespassing on Cordy's property. That's why he'd dragged me there. Just like he'd dragged me to meet Esme, whom we'd both fallen hard for.

"Garnet, great to meet you," I said in my best *I am suave* voice.

She turned bright pink, which *really* made my dick twitch, and let her hand linger in mine for a moment. I glanced at Win, who wore one of his big 'happy smirks.'

Win and I moved our stools so we could squeeze another between us.

"Tom?" she said, waving toward the bartender after she'd taken a seat between us. "Can I have a Stella?"

"So, you're a Stella girl, huh?" I asked.

She took a sip of her beer. "Yeah. Love Stella."

She looked at the two of us. "So, how long you guys been friends? How do you know each other?"

"We went to elementary school together," Win answered, nodding. Those were not happy days for either of us, but I liked to think that was all behind us now.

"It has been a *long* time that I've known this jerk," I added, holding up my beer to him. "Cheers, buddy."

Garnet joined us. Bottles clicked all around.

"To new friends," Win said.

Her face lit up with a huge—and may I say gorgeous—crooked smile.

"You two have known each other since you were kids? I have that with my friend Matty. It's really something to have known someone for so long."

"So Brose, what restaurant are you working in?" she asked.

"North by Northwest. Also known to regulars as NbN," I said.

"Get out! I've never been there but have heard it's all the rage right now. That's so cool."

"Maybe you can come in sometime. I'm the sous chef there. We have a slamming menu. You'd like it."

I couldn't help but brag about the place. I'd worked in a lot of restaurants during my training, but never one like this.

Win piped up. "Brose's real dream is to have his own restaurant some day. Just wait 'til you try his cooking."

She looked between the two of us. Could she already know what we were thinking?

"What are we waiting for? We should go right now." She threw her head back for another one of her beautiful laughs.

"Why not?" I asked.

I could see myself walking through the door with this gorgeous, down to earth woman on my arm.

Cripes, what was wrong with me? I'd just met her.

Chill the fuck out, dude.

"I was just kidding. For one, I am supposed to be working in," she looked at her watch, "four minutes. Let's do it another time. And you guys are welcome to hang out. Hell, if you're nice to me, I may even give you a free beer or two."

I looked at Win, and we laughed. Did this woman know us, or what?

Garnet hustled over behind the bar and got to work, serving the customers who were just arriving, greeting them like long-lost friends.

"So," Win said to me.

"So, yourself," I said back.

"You enjoying your fancy beer?" he asked, his head tilting toward my Sierra.

"Yup. You enjoying your shitty beer?"

"Yup."

A few silent minutes slipped by. Without meaning to, we both watched Garnet smiling and laughing as she did her thing.

I broke the quiet.

"I don't know about her leasing the house, but I definitely would like to get to know her better. How do you feel about that?" I asked.

Win looked at me and nodded slowly. We'd navigated

this before. Women were not something we fought about. We'd been through too much together, and our friendship was much more important than getting our rocks off.

"She's a cool girl. What do you say we each go out with her and see how she feels about things?"

"It's a plan," I said, watching her gorgeous ass hustle from one end of the bar to the other.

9

GARNET

"Hey, it's about time you got your ass out of bed," Matty shrieked at me over the phone, waking me from a dead sleep.

"Matty. I closed last night. I didn't get home 'til two a.m. I should at least be able to sleep until nine-thirty or ten. And don't you have work to do, anyway?"

I needed a cushy receptionist job like he had, where I could gab on the phone half the day with my friends and cruise online dating sites the other half.

I pushed myself to sitting, stuffing pillows behind me. The usual San Francisco fog billowed past my window, socking in the city.

"So have you spoken to the lawyer?" he asked. "What's the latest on Grandpa's estate?"

"Nothing new. Mr. Jones told me to call him if I found a husband. How ridiculous is that?"

Honestly, I couldn't believe he'd even talked to me about that with a straight face.

"Is he single, by any chance?"

That was my Matty. Always looking for his next lay.

"I have no idea, nor do I know if he even plays for your team. But somehow, I think that would be a massive conflict of interest. Anyway, I'm thinking I might have found some husband prospects."

That sounded so creepy.

He sucked his breath in with interest. "Seriously? Prospects? With an 's' on the end, like plural?"

"Yeah, can you believe it? I mean, maybe I'm imagining things, but who knows. The first guy is Nat, the accountant the lawyer put me in touch with. He's blond, sort of a preppy Ralph Lauren-looking guy. I told you about him already. He's kind of uptight and seems to work really hard."

"Oh my god. Marry him so I can look at him at Thanksgiving and Christmas dinner! He sounds delicious," Matty squealed.

"Down boy," I said. "Then there's Linc, the guy who owns the gym with his brother. He's tall and buff, seems shy, but is super sweet. He's the one who rescued me from that Craigslist creep."

"Ohhh, right. He's sounds like a god. Maybe he has a big d—"

"C'mon Matty. I'm trying to be serious here."

Big sigh, followed by a big huff.

"Okay," I continued. "Then there are two guys who are

friends. Win reminds me of the Marlboro Man with his craggy, tan face. He's the groundskeeper at Grandpa's mansion, and his best friend, Brose, a gorgeous bald, black guy with a neck tattoo and pierced ears, is a chef at North by Northwest."

"Damn, that's like an encyclopedia of men. I'll take your leftovers if any of them want to try a walk on the wild side."

"I'll be sure to let them know, Matty." I stretched, dragging my butt out of bed. "It would be nice if things worked out but c'mon, how likely is it that anyone finds someone to marry in thirty days? Seriously."

Why did Grandpa fuck me up like this?

"Are you gonna tell them about the money?"

"Hell no. I already tried being up front about the money with that stupid Craigslist ad and look what happened. I attracted every creep in the Bay Area."

"Then how the hell are you going to get one of them to marry you by the end of the month?"

"I don't know. What would you do if you were me?"

He cackled. "I know exactly what I'd do. I'd go out with all of them and pick the guy with the biggest dick!"

That's my Matty. But he had a point.

I WALKED to work to clear my head and ended up getting

there early. On the way, I passed my usual posse of homeless buddies and stopped to say hi to them.

"Hey, Tom," I said, grabbing a seat at the bar when I'd arrived. Since we were in between lunch and happy hour, the place was empty. While I liked the bar when it was hopping with activity, it was also kind of magical when it was quiet, like it was waiting for the explosion of activity that was just around the corner.

"Hey, sweetie," he said as he filled the cooler with bottles of beer. "Seems like you've had a busy social life lately."

Damn. Was it that obvious? "You know how it is, when it rains, it pours." I laughed as nonchalantly as I could force myself to. Shit, did he know about Grandpa and the money?

"Yeah, you got yourself some suitors."

I shrugged. "I guess. We'll see what comes of it."

He leaned onto the bar before me. "What else is going on? Still thinking about that sommelier course?"

I sighed deeply. I'd been trying not to think about it, but with Grandpa's money, I might be able to finally make my dream happen.

"I do think about it. A lot. Probably too much."

"What? How can you be thinking about your dream too much?"

I felt a lump growing in my throat. Tom was right. What was wrong with letting yourself have dreams?

In spite of myself, my voice cracked. "You're right. I need to give myself permission to want more than this." I gestured throughout the bar. "Not that there's anything wrong with this."

"Garnet. There is nothing wrong with wanting more than the Drive By Saloon. In fact, I think there would be something wrong with *not* wanting more." The compassion on his face made the tears flow. Thank goodness no patrons had arrived yet.

He came around the bar and took a seat next to me.

"Hey, what's going on?" He put an arm around my shoulder. He and his wife were like a big brother and sister to me.

I wiped my nose on a bar napkin. "Sorry, Tom. I just have a lot going on. It's going to be fine, though, really."

He pulled me into a hug. "Hey, why don't you come by the house sometime soon? I know Ingrid would love to see you."

"Thank you, Tom. You guys are so good to me." They really were.

The first happy hour customers began to trickle in. We weren't busy enough yet for me to get to work so Tom served them. It was going to be a busy night, and I wanted to save my feet for as long as possible.

When I finally joined him behind the bar, I saw Grandpa's seat occupied by a new person. It felt strange.

"Hey, Tom, remember that old guy who used to sit at the end of the bar, the one we called Grandpa?"

"Sure. The one who always kept to himself?"

"And was a lousy tipper," we both said in unison.

"Well, he passed away," I said.

"Oh, I didn't know that. How'd you find out?"

Shit, now I'd done it. "Um…I can't remember. Someone must have told me."

"Well, that's a shame. Hopefully he had a good life. Now, are you ready to get to work? Because I've been here for hours and am exhausted."

"Step aside."

NAT WASN'T PICKING me up for another hour, but I was ready anyway. It wasn't like me to be ahead of schedule, but it was so seldom I had a date, I was a wreck. Not that I would ever let on. If I could help it.

The sensation was so odd. How could I be nervous about a date with a freaking accountant.

Was he going to talk about balance sheets and shit like that?

I was wearing a nice fitted wrap top that accentuated my shape, as well as the comfortable shoes he'd suggested I wear. Why he recommended footwear for our outing, I wasn't sure, but I guess I'd find out. Anyway, I'd gotten a new MAC lipstick, curled my hair with my wand, and actually felt pretty freaking good.

While I had time to kill, Tom's words at the bar drifted back to me—that if my only ambition was to stay at the Drive By 'til the end of my days, then I was selling myself short. I'd always been fascinated by wine and wanted to learn more. I flipped open my laptop and Googled sommelier courses. The amount of information was insane.

There were several levels to advance through, starting with introductory courses. But damn, it was all so expensive. The beginner courses started around six hundred dollars and the advanced ones were upwards of two thousand. On top of that steep price tag, to progress, there were what looked like very hard tests. You could get *certified*, pass to the *advanced* level, and if you were really ambitious, become a *master*. And I found that fewer than twenty-five percent of sommeliers are women. What was up with that?

I clicked my laptop closed. What was the point? With the student loans I was trying to pay off, the cost of the sommelier courses, and the tests that looked impossible to pass, who was I fooling? I was no sooner going to become a master sommelier than I was a millionaire living in a mansion overlooking San Francisco Bay.

10

NAT

I swung by Garnet's place in the Mission to pick her up for our date. I had to admit, I'd really been looking forward to seeing her again, something that rarely happened for me.

I was still puzzled about our meeting. I mean, wasn't it odd that she had wanted to talk about accounting matters when, from what I could see, the girl didn't have a pot to piss in? And why had Jonesy sent me to her? But she was hot as hell, and her crooked smile slayed me. So, all was not lost.

I double-parked in the street like everyone else in San Francisco did and rang her bell. Holy Christ, she took my breath away when she came to the door. She had this long, wavy-curly hair that almost didn't look real, and her bright blue eyes glowed. Yeah, there was something about her that was magical. I couldn't put my finger on it, but it felt good.

"You look amazing," I said, opening the passenger side of my car for her.

Damn if I wasn't already getting hard in my jeans. I helped myself to her hand as we drove across town. If she wiggled out of my grip, I'd know her level of interest. But good news—she took my fingers just as tightly as I held hers.

"So, where we goin'?" she asked.

"You'll see," I teased. I stole a look and found her smiling. For the longest time I'd been avoiding getting into any sort of relationship in order to concentrate on my career, but I could sure as hell see myself spending time with this woman.

We pulled into a parking spot in the Fisherman's Wharf neighborhood, and I grabbed her hand again to lead her through the throngs of tourists.

"Hmmm. I don't know if I should just be following you," she joked. "You know, with no idea of where we're going."

"Maybe you shouldn't," I shot back.

I led her down a dock toward a small sailboat. A captain walked out of the hull as we approached.

"No way!" she said, turning to me with wide-open eyes. "We're going sailing? I've never been on a sailboat."

I held her hand as she stepped aboard. Before I knew it, the captain had untied us from the dock and we were underway.

We settled onto the bench seat in the stern. I reached into a bucket to pull out a bottle of champagne.

"Thirsty?" I asked.

"Yes, please." Her eyes were wide, and she stared up at the sky. "Wow, look at the full moon. It's incredible. And so quiet."

"I thought you might like it."

She looked directly at me. "Thank you. This is amazing."

It wasn't a particularly windy night, so we sailed across the Bay at a mellow clip. It was perfect for someone who'd never been sailing before. Heck, I'd been only a few times myself.

"So how long have you worked for the accounting firm?" she asked.

"Six years. I have great clients, but I work long hours. I'd like to pull back a bit, but I'm at the stage where I could make partner in the next year."

"Really? Is it worth it? Or will you just have to work even harder?" she asked.

"The irony is that, while I'd take on more responsibility, my hours would not be longer. And I'd get paid a lot more."

I could just make out her features in the moonlight, with her hair whipping in the breeze. Damn if she didn't smell great, all simple soap and shampoo.

My job was about the last thing I wanted to be talking about.

"What drives you so hard?" she asked.

"Well, I didn't have much growing up, so I'm working

for some security. But sometimes, I wonder how much is enough. You know what I mean?"

"I do. I do know what you mean," she said, nodding.

"Garnet?" I asked.

"Yes?"

I leaned toward her. "I'm going to kiss you now." I wrapped my fingers in a fistful of her hair and drew her toward me, touching lips that were as delicious as I knew they'd be. I let my fingers trail down the front of her blouse, where they landed on a magnificent breast topped with a very hard nipple. Shit, if I wasn't careful, I'd explode right there in my pants.

I eventually looked up to see the captain had gotten us back to the dock. How the hell had two hours passed so quickly?

"Thanks for the sail, it was great," I said.

"You're very welcome." He tied us to the dock and left.

"Wait," she said, standing. "Where's he going? Don't we have to get off the boat too?"

"Sit back down." I pulled her to the seat. "I've got the boat for the night. We can hang out as long as we want, right here in the slip."

"No way. This is fantastic." She leaned back on the bench and stared up at the sky. "What's that tinkling sound? It's so pretty."

"Those are the buckles that connect to the sails. I call it boat music." The sound always made me happy. "I hope to have a sailboat of my own someday. But for now, I'll just have to hire them when I want to go out."

I stood and pulled her to me. "Why don't we go check out the stateroom?"

"What's that?" She stood and shyly took my hand.

"It's a fancy name for a bedroom on a boat. Watch your head," I told her. We ducked beneath a low door, taking a few steps down to below decks.

"Oh my god, look at this." She did a complete three-sixty to take in the room with its polished wood and king-size bed.

"Garnet," I said slowly, running my hand along the soft skin of her arm.

I grasped her fingers, bringing them to my cheek. Her reaction to my touch was just what I'd hoped for. Everything about her was new. I'd known few women who were beautiful and smart, confident and ambitious. And at the same time, vulnerable. Which made me mad with passion. Fuck, I wanted her.

I ran my fingers up the back of her neck and drew her to me. Unable to wait a second longer, I embraced her with everything I had. Those damn pillow-soft lips seared into mine, and when my tongue sought entrance into her mouth, she whimpered like she'd not been properly kissed in a long time. Strangely, time stood still *and* sped up as we got lost in a kiss before we pulled apart, gasping for air as the boat rocked lightly in its slip.

Holy shit.

Her face was flushed with need that I was only too happy to fill, and she drew her fingers up to her lips as if she expected them to be bruised from our encounter.

"Garnet, I've been wanting to do that since the first time I saw you, the day I came to the bar," I whispered.

She fell into a smile so beautiful, it nearly broke my heart. At the same time, my cock bounced to full attention, straining against my blue jeans and causing me more than a little pain.

"Really?" she giggled nervously.

I looked at every inch of her face. "How did you not know? Are you unaware of how fucking amazing you are?"

I kissed her again, ferociously this time. I lifted her, bringing her to the bed where I laid her back and inched between her legs, our blue jeans grinding against each other, out of place and unwelcome.

"May I?" I asked, my fingers poised on the fly of her jeans.

She lay back on the bed, her eyes partially closed, her hair splayed over the comforter like a goddess. My goddess.

"Mmmm," she murmured, rolling her head back and forth. "Yes," she breathed.

I got her jeans open and down to her hips where I laid my eyes on a tiny lace thong that I knew I'd like a whole lot more when it was in my teeth, being dragged off her lovely bottom.

As soon as she was naked from the waist down, her hand flew to her clit, where she began to make small circles. Goddamn if I didn't love a woman who didn't hesitate to beat off right in front of me. If you asked me, nothing was hotter.

I ran my palms up the inside of her thighs, drawing out the inevitable moment when I would no longer be able to restrain myself. I groaned as I drank in the scent of her excitement—a fresh pussy dying for attention, dripping onto the bed below. I pushed her hand aside to press my own thumb to her clit. When I made the lightest of circles, she moaned and lifted her hips to give me more access.

And when I finally tasted her, I went into a free fall, my world rocked from right under my feet. Fortunately, she was on the edge of the bed so I could kneel—I no longer trusted my legs to keep me upright. She was salty, sweet, and fresh, her pussy quivering and begging for more. Slipping a finger into my mouth, I wet it and slowly worked it into her tight core, which gripped me with a hunger I'd underestimated. My girl from the Drive By Saloon needed me and my touch. I was going to give her everything she ever wanted.

And then some.

11

GARNET

Good god, had it been a long time since I'd been with a guy, much less a *man* like Nat. Sure, I felt the rush of reservations about messing around with a guy I hardly knew, but it was happening, and it was intense and magical and there was no way in hell I'd stop it. Don't ask me how I knew, but it was more than sex. Our connection was fast and strong.

Sometimes, it just happened that way.

I wasn't usually drawn to the super-straight preppy sort of dude, but Nat's kiss had me all twisted up inside. Each one took me further away from any assumptions I had that an accountant couldn't be anything more than a bore. How wrong that was, I was happy to find.

"Oh, god," I cried as he felt inside me with his thick fingers, reaching my g-spot and bringing me to the edge of what would be the first of many orgasms.

"You're so fucking wet, baby," he growled as his lips

found my hard clit again. The suction drove me wild, leaving me thrashing on the edge of the stateroom's bed. I could have sworn I was causing the boat to rock. Maybe I was.

"You doing okay?" he asked, checking in.

"God yes," I managed to choke, gasping as he fucked me harder with his fingers. I planted my feet on the end of the bed for leverage and lifted my hips to drive further onto him. But before I could come, he shifted, and in an instant was over my body, hands under my blouse, lips running down my temple to my neck and back up again. He slipped a finger into my mouth and watched me enjoy my own tang.

"God, I've wanted to get my hands on your delicious tits," he said when he'd pushed up my shirt and moved my bra out of the way.

His fingers flamed my sensitive skin, leaving me writhing with a touch I couldn't decide whether to call pain or pleasure. Maybe because it was a combination of the two. His mouth found my nipples, licking and biting them as he ground his hard erection through his abrasive jeans against my bare, soaked pussy. I cried out from the rough fabric, but I had to admit, I pressed harder into him for more. All I could think of was *how I wanted more.*

He dropped back to his crouch, his face positioned right between my legs. His tongue wandered up my thigh, alternating with small nibbles, until he reached my wet and puffy lips. He pushed my legs even wider apart and ran his face up and down, from my ass to my clit, with long, deep strokes of his tongue.

The orgasm that had been building hit me like a truck, but he didn't slow. His relentless mouth brought me to another, leaving me gulping for air, every nerve in my body screaming in response. As I struggled to raise my head to see him, I found him yanking at his belt buckle and slipping his jeans and boxers down his thighs. I was so woozy, I could barely think about what was next.

He took a step back, finally giving me a full view of his hard pecs, tight abs, and the perfect line of hair that ran from his belly button to a very hard and delicious-looking cock. I nearly passed out watching him run his hand up and down his long erection, stroking slowly and deliberately, his gaze locked on mine. As I came back to my senses, I pushed myself up to sitting and removed what was left of the clothes hanging off my body. With a good look at Nat, my energy came rushing back. I stood from the bed and moved toward him with an extended hand, his gaze wandering over my naked body. I positioned him on the edge of the bed where I'd just been and lowered myself to between his knees.

I took his cock out of his hand and ran my fingers over the velvety shaft. His head was too wide to close my grip around, so I loosened my fingers and gathered the first drop of precum to my mouth. It was salty and sweet.

"Fuck baby, I like how you stroke me," he growled. "Give me some more."

I smiled at him, slowly moving my mouth toward his

erection. I ran my tongue over the glistening head of his cock, enclosing my lips around it and creating a light suction while I tasted him. He dropped his head back, muttering something incomprehensible. But I think I knew what he was getting at.

I lowered my head over his cock until it banged the back of my throat. My eyes watered, but I couldn't stop. He tasted so good, and I wanted to make him feel as great as he'd made me. I pistoned my lips up and down his length from root to tip, keeping my eyes locked with his.

Reaching my free hand between my legs, I found myself creamy and dripping and ran my fingers up and down the slickness between my puffy lips. My hand and mouth worked in perfect rhythm together and another orgasm was building for me, just as one was for Nat.

He bucked his hips against my greedy mouth, and when he saw me pounding my pussy, I could swear he got even stiffer. With my free hand, I grabbed his balls and gave a gentle tug, which sent him into a frenzy. Just as I'd hoped.

"Uh…I'm coming…god I'm coming," he shouted.

The room filled with my own cries as the white heat of climax shot over and through me.

As soon as I had the strength, I scooted up on the bed next to him. He drew a comforter over us, and with my head buried in his shoulder, we dozed.

The morning sun splashed across the stateroom, waking me from a sound sleep, alone and at first, unsure of where I was. When the gentle rock of the boat made itself known, I remembered where I'd fallen asleep, and why I had a smile on my face. I turned to see Nat coming down the steps from the deck shirtless, in his jeans.

"Hey, baby. Went outside for some fresh air. Gorgeous day."

I sat up in the bed, the comforter falling down to my waist. Nat looked at my breasts with hunger.

"Do you need to use the bathroom? The head's over there," he said, pointing at a small, closed door. "There are towels and anything else you might need."

I scooted over to the bathroom—or *head*, as I guessed they called it on a boat—feeling Nat's eyes burning on my backside until I pulled the door closed behind me. I didn't mind. My backside was good-sized with plenty of curve. I had no complaints. Spending all day on my feet, squatting and bending behind the bar to get glasses and bottles was one of the best workouts a girl could have.

The boat's bathroom was tiny, with just enough room for a shower stall, a toilet, and a sink. But it was paneled in beautiful dark wood and the floor was covered in shiny white tiles. There was a shelf loaded with fluffy towels, so I grabbed one and splashed my face with water. My complexion was nice and pink from the events of the night before, and I noticed my mouth was a little puffy from Nat's enthusiastic kissing. I finger-combed my hair to remove some of the knots but had to say that, in spite having spent the night in a strange bed, I felt freaking great.

"Hey, baby," I said to Nat as I opened the bathroom door. He'd crawled back into bed, leaving his pants on the floor in a puddle with my clothes. The place was a delicious mess with champagne flutes, shoes, underwear, and other articles of dress scattered about. Signs of a good time.

He pulled back the edge of the comforter, gesturing for me to get back in. Before I knew it, he'd positioned me so I was on top of him in a straddle, with him tweaking my nipples while he pulled me down to kiss him. I felt his hard cock pressing against my leg and decided I wasn't done with him, not by a long shot.

"Nat," I breathed, "do you have a condom?"

"I do, baby." He reached for his pants on the floor and dug into one of his pockets.

"Guess you were feeling optimistic?" I teased.

"Hey, you can't blame a guy for hoping," he said with a laugh.

He moved me just enough to position the condom over his cock, and when he was sheathed, gazed up at me.

"You ready, baby? You ready for my cock?"

"I don't know, Nat," I breathed, his filthy words

causing me to shake. I jutted out my bottom lip to play coy. "It seems kind of big."

"Well then, we'll go nice and slow. I promise you'll like it. You'll like it deep inside you."

I was convinced.

He reached for my ass and lifted me so I hovered just above him. He rubbed his tip against my hard clit.

"I'm taking your pretty pussy, baby."

He opened my lips with two fingers and entered me a half-inch or so, giving me time to adjust to the wide head of his cock. Then he bounced me on it another inch or so, very lightly, to spread my moisture. I was turned on as hell, ready to fucking explode, especially at the way he was taking his time with me. It must have been torture for him.

He thumbed my clit as I slowly engulfed him, and damn if I wasn't quickly crammed full of his cock, stretched nearly to my limit. My head dropped back while I ground myself on him, and his hands flew to my breasts to pull and squeeze my nipples. The pleasure/pain sensation was overwhelming—almost more than I could take. I heard a grunting and groaning sound in the room, and realized it was me.

When he was completely seated inside me, he thrust his hips to drive even deeper with powerful, unforgiving attacks. I held on to his chest for balance and rode him as hard as I could.

"I want to feel you come," he growled between

clenched teeth, his gaze locked with mine. It was so *intimate*, I thought I might crawl out of my skin.

"I'm coming now," I whispered. I couldn't manage anything more. "Fuck me, keep fucking me, please," I murmured.

My whole body began to shake, and my breath came in gasps. My pussy throbbed around him, his moans filling the stateroom. He drove into me again and again, and when he fingered my clit, it was all over. Yet another orgasm crashed into me. My head dropped to my chest, and I went limp. Nat took over, and holding me up, and drove into me one last time before he pulled me to him, exhausted, sweaty, and buzzing with burning heat.

After a few minutes' recovery, I lifted my head from his shoulder.

"I never knew accountants could be so hot," I told him, running kisses over the side of his handsome face.

He gave me a naughty grin. "You have a lot to learn about accountants."

12

LINC

I'd been looking forward to seeing Garnet in my gym, and when she walked in, I immediately remembered why. Her stretchy workout clothes left little to the imagination, hugging her curvy hips and nice, full breasts.

Stop staring, asshole.

"Linc! How ya doing?" she asked.

I wiped my sweaty palms on the sides of my gym pants and took a deep breath. I'd never had much luck with the ladies, and I didn't want to blow this one. I rarely asked girls out, and when I did, I often ended up tongue-tied. No one wanted to date a guy who couldn't carry on a conversation. My brother gave me hell about it, but he didn't know shit. It really *was* hell.

"I'm glad you came. I've been wanting to show you around," I said.

"Well, thank you for inviting me." She clearly had no shyness problem. I suppose you had to be outgoing if you were a bartender, talking to people all day. Actually, I spoke to people all day, too, but I answered more questions than had actual conversations—*Where's the weight room? How do I sign up for yoga?*

I led her up the stairs. "Come check out the office."

Since we'd opened the place in an old warehouse, we'd had pretty much free rein in how we wanted to build it out. There was a reception desk by the front door, but the office I shared with Jack was on a mezzanine where we could overlook most of what was going on in the gym. It was a great way to keep an eye on things. Of course, my brother used it to scope chicks.

"Wow, this view is awesome." Garnet moved from overlooking the basketball courts, to the swimming pool, to the weight rooms.

"There are group exercise rooms too, but we can't see them from here."

"How much is membership? I might like to join," she asked.

Was she kidding? I wasn't going to take her money.

"I'm not charging you."

She smiled. "What? You have to charge me, you're a growing business. I *want* to pay."

"Tell you what. Give me a free beer every now and then and we'll be square."

She raised her hands in surrender. "Okay, okay. It's a deal."

I don't know what it was, but I felt so damn comfortable with her. It made no sense. I didn't even know her.

"Let's go sweat a bit, yeah?" I asked.

"Ugh. Please don't kick my butt," she begged.

"We'll see about that. How about we start with the treadmill?"

There were two free ones where we could jog side by side.

I got her started at not much more than a brisk walk and showed her how to increase the speed when she felt ready. I'd already done my cardio for the day, but a little extra wouldn't hurt.

"So, when did you say you guys opened the place?" she asked, slightly winded.

I had to think for a moment. "Geez. Almost a year now. I can't believe it's been that long."

As she picked up speed on the treadmill, I could smell her lush hair. It was a simple scent, not much more than clean shampoo. And it was amazing.

Her face was beginning to glisten, and I caught a look at her bouncing breasts. I felt a twitch in my pants, something that had not happened in a long time.

"Are you and your brother close?"

I nodded. "We are. I mean, we're really different from each other. He's gregarious, and I'm more on the quiet side. But we've been through a lot."

I wondered if I should share more. Oh, what the hell.

"We grew up in foster care, so most times we only had each other. We had to stick together."

"Did you grow up around here?" she asked.

"Yup. Right here in San Francisco."

"What was it like? Growing up in a foster home?"

"You know, I think we got pretty lucky. I mean, some of the places were great, some not so great. But we didn't end up in any bad places like some kids do. Still, you have to move around a lot, switch schools, and so forth. You get really good at fighting. We were a team then. Guess we still are."

She'd increased the speed on her treadmill by another small increment and was handling it well. She was a strong girl, which I was glad to see. Not a silly, vain thing like some of the women who came to work out.

"It must be nice to have a sibling. I am an only child. Raised by my mom. Who didn't really want to be a mom."

"I hear that," I said, thinking back over my own situation.

We got off the treadmills and, grabbing water, sank into seats in the lounge area.

"Thank you again for rescuing me from that creep. I really appreciate it."

Christ, even her sweat smelled great.

"It was my pleasure. He was clearly assaulting you. He'd better not come by the bar again."

"Geez, I hope not. Unless you happen to be there," she said with a laugh, shaking her head. "So much for online dating."

"Don't you meet people at the bar?"

She shrugged and shook her head. "Not really. You know, most of them are old timers, regulars who've been going there forever. Besides, work is not the best place to look for dates, you know?"

"Try telling that to my brother. He chases every pretty girl who walks in here. I keep telling him to watch it, but he never does."

It was nearing closing time and the gym was clearing out.

"C'mon, let's go back to the office," I said.

We ran right into Jack.

"Garnet!" he said, giving her a big bear hug. "How's my favorite bartender?" He always knew exactly what to say. He stepped back to discreetly check her out. She didn't even notice, but I knew him, and how he operated. I had to admit, I felt a twinge of jealousy at his easy way with her. But I knew he'd never go for a woman I was interested in. That was where he drew the line.

"Jack, good to see you. Come by the bar sometime," she told him.

He looked at me. "Linc, how come we haven't been by the bar in a while?"

"Cuz Jack, we've been working like dogs. But Garnet's right, we need to get over there more often."

Just then, the office door flew open.

It was our receptionist. "Hey, I just made the rounds and it looks like everyone's gone. I'm gonna head out, okay?"

Jack stood to leave. "I'm outta here, too. I'm exhausted. Linc, will you close up on your way out?"

"Yup. Just lock the door behind yourselves," I said.

When they were gone, I offered Garnet a beer from the small fridge we kept in the corner. I opened two and handed her one.

"Cheers," she said, and we clinked bottles. "You guys should be really proud of yourselves." She waved a hand, encompassing the view below. "You've accomplished a heck of a lot. The club is freaking gorgeous, and it's in a great location. You're going to be hugely successful. I just know it."

It was nice to get a vote of confidence. "Thank you. We've worked our asses off. I hope like hell you're right."

"I know I am," she said with a tilted head and a small smile. That was all I needed. I'd been dying to kiss her for two damn hours. So, I leaned in for the kill.

Her lips were soft and tasty, like I knew they'd be, and she eagerly accepted mine. I slowed until my lips were barely touching hers and realized her breaths were coming long and hard, like mine were starting to.

"Garnet, you taste so good," I murmured against her mouth.

She responded with a light moan.

Even though she was a tall girl, I towered over her and had to bend down to reach her mouth. She melted into me in a perfect fit, and I felt myself fully erect in my gym pants, where a raging hard-on was not easy to hide. But maybe it didn't need to be hidden.

I took Garnet's beer from her and set it with mine on my brother's desk. Then I turned her around and pressed her against the large window overlooking the room below.

She gasped. "Can anyone see us up here?"

"Nope. The other side of the glass is mirrored. Besides, we're the only ones left." She relaxed, arching her back so her butt pressed hard into my cock. Jesus, if I didn't watch it, I'd come right there.

I placed her hands on the glass in front of her for leverage, and from my position behind her, reached around to catch her hanging breasts. They more than filled my hands, which about drove me crazy. Nothing like big tits and an ass.

"You good?" I whispered in her ear.

She responded with an enthusiastic nod.

Emboldened, I reached under her workout top and pushed aside her jog bra. I finally had my hands on her bare flesh. Her nipples jumped to attention as I squeezed and kneaded them, and when I pinched harder, she let out the hottest freaking moan I'd ever heard.

13

GARNET

Good lord, it was amazing to have a big, strong man's hands on me. I closed my eyes and pretended people could see me through the window Linc had me pressed against. I'd never thought of myself as an exhibitionist, but then, I'd never made out with a guy in front of a window, either.

In my forward-bent position, I could feel his cock pressing into the crack of my behind, which scared me into thinking what it might be like to have that huge thing inside me. But those thoughts drifted away as Linc's hands worked over my tits. Damn if he didn't have the magic touch, and when he reached my bare flesh and began torturing my nipples, my legs quaked to the point of collapse. But the glass wall in front of me, and Linc and his giant cock behind me, were keeping me upright.

It passed through my mind for about a second that I'd

been with Nat only the night before. Did that make me a slut?

Ugh, I hated that ridiculous type of thinking. If a guy was with different women two nights in a row, he'd be a goddamn hero. Why wouldn't I be the same?

Besides, I was on a mission. I had less than three weeks at this point to find someone to marry or I might be working in the lovable but dumpy Drive By Saloon til the end of my days.

I couldn't let that happen.

Next thing I knew, my leggings were being eased below my ass. I wiggled my hips to help them down, and Linc stopped just below the crack of my butt. He crouched and buried his face right in my ass, taking a deep breath.

I can't say anyone had ever done that to me before, but it was a massive turn on to know someone could get so worked up over my fleshy behind. I'd never felt more desired than in that moment.

After another inhale, he mumbled, "Your ass is fucking sweet."

My leggings were now down to my ankles, and he helped me step out of them after I'd kicked off my sneakers. He pushed my feet apart and bent me further, so I was at a ninety degree angle with my ass sticking up in the air. I'd never been so exposed in a public place. Someone could walk in at any moment, regardless that Linc said everyone was gone. How could he know? The place was huge, and surely, there was a janitor or someone finishing his work.

But I was rapidly getting to where I didn't give a shit. My new position left me wide open, and his tongue found the rosebud of my ass so fast, I nearly jumped through the window I was leaning on.

I'd never been into anal, not even wanted to experiment or try it, but I had to say, Linc's tongue was driving me to insanity. Still, with what I suspected was the huge cock he dragged around between his legs, he wasn't sticking that where I bet he wanted to.

As if he'd read my mind, he reached between my legs with two fingers and dragged them along my soaked pussy lips. I ground into his hand for more stimulation, and when I did, his finger slipped right inside me.

He stood up from his crouch, keeping his finger seated in me. He bent forward over my back and grabbed me by the waist as if he were going to lift me. But he just held me tight. Then, he starting finger fucking me faster, and the wetter I got and the louder I moaned, the harder he gave it to me. Shit, at that point, I wouldn't have cared if he shoved his giant cock up my ass, I was in such ecstasy.

Linc held me immobile from behind, and I started to scream as he pushed me over the edge of orgasm.

"You coming, sweetie? You gonna come for me?" he growled in my ear.

Damn if it didn't come as a surprise that Linc was a dirty-talker, and damn if I wasn't thrilled about it.

I screamed through another orgasm, this time unable

to catch my breath. My legs shook first, then it was my whole body. Good thing Linc was there with his big arm around my waist, because he ended up holding me like I was a ragdoll. Everything in the room went black.

I CAME TO, laid out on the floor of the office. He'd pulled a fleece blanket over me and gotten a cool towel for my forehead.

"Hi," I said weakly.

"I think I finger-banged you into oblivion."

"You did. Wow." I pushed myself to sit up, and Linc caught me with a hand behind my back.

"Take it slow, cowgirl," he said, handing me a cup of water.

My head cleared quickly, and I remembered we had unfinished business. For one, Linc was still fully dressed.

Time for me to take charge.

When the cobwebs were gone, I removed what was left of my clothing—a jog bra, yoga top, and leggings, still dangling from my foot. I knelt on the blanket and gazed up. God, he was gorgeous with his evening scruff and tousled shoulder-length hair. I lowered the zip on his track jacket and threw that aside. Then I reached for his T-shirt with the gym's name emblazoned across it. I removed that too, and when I got a load of his chest, I could scarcely breathe.

His shoulders and pecs were like small mountains, and his rocky biceps were surrounded by tattoos of something tribal-looking. I caught my breath as I followed his perfect splay of chest hair along the line that ran down the center of his muscled abdomen. It ended far below the waistband of his sweats, but I was planning to get there in due time.

But before I could, Linc hooked a finger under my chin and pulled my mouth up to meet his. This time, his kiss was more aggressive, and I felt myself swelling with need again. I lowered his pants, leaving him only in his boxer briefs. I couldn't see the prize, but the outline of it was pretty freaking amazing.

"Would you mind standing, please?" I asked him.

Without a word, he was towering above me, gazing down. From my kneeling position, I hooked my fingers into his waistband and slowly began to lower the last article of clothing he wore.

Of course, they got hung up on the giant hard-on in front of my face. I widened the waistband to make room for his cock, finally able to lay my eyes on it in person.

And good lord, I'd never seen anything like it. First, it was so fat, my fingers couldn't close around it, not by a long shot.

Could he actually fuck with that?

He must have noticed my shock. "Yeah, I know, it's big. Sometimes it's a good thing, and sometimes it's not." He smiled. "But don't worry. I know how to use it."

I must have turned bright red because fire washed

over my face. I hated it when my tendency to blush gave away my emotions. Besides, I'd already been pretty intimate with this guy—I wasn't sure why the hell I'd be embarrassed, but something about him was sweet and maybe even a little vulnerable.

I wanted him to like me.

"Well, it's beautiful," I purred, extending my tongue for a taste of his precum.

"Mmmm," he crooned, letting his eyes close.

He held his heavy cock from its base, as if he were offering it to me. I stretched my mouth as wide as it would allow and engulfed as much of him as I could.

"Oh, fuck," he hollered, throwing his head back. "Goddamn, sweetie, that feels great."

I began to piston my mouth over him, my cheeks hollowing from the suction. He put his hands on my head, grabbing fistfuls of my hair, gently rocking his hips to meet my thrusts. I grabbed his muscular thighs for balance—I could no longer see clearly because my eyes were tearing. But I couldn't stop my hunger.

I relaxed my throat to avoid gagging. I wanted to take him deeper, or at least as deep as I possibly could. His moans sent a jolt through my body, electrified with the knowledge that I could bring him so much pleasure. Every nerve ending of mine was firing overtime, leaving my clit hanging heavy between my legs.

While I worked over Linc, I reached for my pussy and found I was soaked down to my inner thighs. Holy shit, what this guy did to me. His cock stiffened in my mouth, and just as I got ready to swallow his load, he pulled out.

"I wanna come on your tits, darlin'. That okay?" he managed to say, hand on cock.

I could only nod, that's how fucking hot I was.

"Give them to me," he growled. "Give me those fucking tits."

I scooped them together just in time to catch the white stream of his cum. He showered me in a flood of hot semen, trembling from the power of his orgasm. My gaze locked with his, and I ran a finger over my nipple to scoop up some of his cum. I popped it in my mouth to savor his taste.

"Goddamn, you're hot," he said.

He lifted me to standing and brought me to his desk. He pushed aside his laptop and some papers and laid me back. He'd grabbed a condom from somewhere, and then he stood, positioned at my soaked entrance.

"Are you ready, sweetie?" He was already hard again. Amazing.

"Yeah. Just go slow."

His gaze was locked with mine as he opened me to make way for his swollen head. The minute I felt him slide in, I gasped at his size. I knew he was huge and that it might be uncomfortable for a moment, but the way he took his time and watched for my reaction was so caring and respectful, I was blown away.

"Take a deep breath," he whispered, his hungry gaze not wavering.

He had one thumb circling my clit, and as he pushed inside me an inch further, the added pressure in my pussy drew me over the edge.

My body convulsed, and I heard myself screaming as my head thrashed and my hips bucked to meet his drives. He watched me come with an expression of happy satisfaction. Before I knew it, he was all the way inside me, and it not only felt good, it felt great—so intense, so full. He leaned toward me, pressing his lips to mine when he released a growl so powerful, for a moment I wondered if he was okay.

"So… good," was all he could manage.

14

WIN

I KNEW.

She didn't. But I did.

I'd be spending a lot of time with Garnet. I knew as soon as she started lying to me. Made no damn sense, I know.

I normally hated liars. Actually, I *always* hated liars. Something about them just seemed so yellow-bellied, and yet...I was ready to let Garnet off the hook. I had no idea why she was bullshitting me the day she came over to scope out Cordy's place, but I could tell from the look on her face, she wouldn't have done it unless she absolutely had to. Something was up with her. I could almost smell fear.

And fear will make you do crazy things. Like when I was about to be busted for pot. I ran, and when I was finally caught, I lied my ass off to get out of trouble. Didn't work, though. Never does.

So whatever was up with her had to be something big. And I wanted to know what it was. And for some inexplicable reason, I wanted to help her. Sure, she was gorgeous with that wild hair and those insane curves, but there was something in her eyes, which were so kind and sincere, that really got under my skin.

That's why I was heading into the city on my motorcycle, in spite of the crappy weather and gale force winds that shook my bike when I crossed the Golden Gate Bridge. I had to see her and know more about her, and nothing was going to stop me.

I parked on the street and headed for my favorite San Francisco bar, Zeitgeist. I'd wanted to get there early so I could watch her come in, but when I pushed open the place's big wooden door, who did I see but my beautiful Garnet, sitting there with a beer, chatting up the bartender.

"Hey, gorgeous," I said, grabbing the stool next to her. She immediately brightened, leading to a twitchy feeling in my jeans.

"Win!" She jumped up to give me a hug, and boy, did she smell nice. "It's great to be in a bar other than the Drive By. I gotta get out more often."

She dropped her head back and laughed. She seemed much more sure of herself than the day I caught her snooping. Understandable, I suppose.

"Well, the Drive By is a pretty cool old bar. There aren't many of those left. My friend Brose enjoyed meeting you, too," I said.

"He was great, really nice guy."

She'd just finished her beer, so I waved the bartender over for another. There was the tiniest amount of foam on her upper lip. I wanted to lick it away so badly, but forced myself to behave. Instead, I used my thumb to wipe it off for her.

"Oh, thank you. Geez, I'm a mess."

"Hardly," I said. I leaned toward her to be heard over the bar's racket. "I'm going to get right to the point here. I really enjoyed meeting you at Cordy's, and then seeing you at the Drive By. I really want to get to know you better."

"Thank you, Win. I feel the same way."

I nodded. I still wanted to know why she lied to me about visiting Cordy's house, but I figured it would eventually come out. I wondered how she'd feel when she knew Brose had every intention of taking her out, too.

"This might sound a bit unorthodox, but Brose would like to… get to know you better, himself."

She looked surprised. Not overly. More like moderately. I took that as a good sign.

"And are you okay with that?" she asked.

I took a swig of my beer and nodded. It would be so freaking awesome if she dug my best friend, too. "Yup. We don't get possessive. We usually like the same things in life, and that often extends to women."

Shit. Was this the part when she'd freak the hell out?

Actually…no.

"Okay. You can give him my number. He seems super cool."

Bingo.

Not wanting to slow the cadence of the evening by making a big deal about the fact that Brose and I liked to share women, I moved on.

"So what's your story? How'd you end up at the Drive By?" I asked.

She gave a big sigh. "I dropped out of college. Never a smart move, but even more stupid when you have piles of student loan debt like I do. At the rate I'm going, I'll be paying on those loans 'til I die." She shook her head. "Anyway, they had a help wanted sign in the window, and I walked by."

"That sucks about the debt. They really do trap you with that student loan business, don't they?"

She nodded, then looked at me. "My real dream is to become a sommelier. Some day."

"Oh yeah? Why are you interested in that?" I asked.

"Well, for one, I love wine and would like to learn more about it. And I think the way it can enhance or ruin a meal is fascinating. But it's also a great career that pays well."

"So what's holding you back?"

She looked down at her beer, and I got another whiff of that sadness—or whatever it was—I'd gotten when we'd first met.

She shrugged her shoulders. "The courses are expensive, and the tests are crazy grueling. I mean, at the end of the master course, you know everything there is to know about wine. Every last thing. Which is so cool."

I spun her on the stool to face me and rested my hands on her knees. "You have to make it happen." As an afterthought, I added, "I think you will."

And the funny thing was, I *knew* she would. Somehow, I knew.

She smiled at my touch, and when I tipped forward to meet her lips, she tilted her head with closed eyes. That was all I needed as evidence she had a hunger inside her. She wanted a lot of things out of life, and while she might feel stuck, I was going to give her what I could—if she let me.

My lips brushed hers, right there in the bar. I didn't care who saw. She put her hands over mine and gripped my fingers, leaving my pulse roaring through my ears. I wasn't sure if her scent was perfume or just shampoo, but I was dying to bury my face in her neck and inhale until she filled every one of my senses.

"Are you trying to seduce me?" she asked.

"I was going to ask if *you* were trying to seduce *me*." Sassy. I liked that. "But would you mind if I were?"

She swallowed, and a pink flush ran over her cheeks. Clearly, I was on the right track. And damn if I didn't want to tear right down that track, right toward shredding off her clothes and tasting her from head to toe. But I could be patient when I had to.

Taking her hand, I threw some money on the bar and jumped off my seat.

"C'mon." I led her toward the back of the bar, past the restrooms and the small kitchen, right out the back door where there was a small seating area for the few people who knew about it. We cut through an opening in the bushes and entered an alley where a couple cars were parked and a bike was locked up. I pressed her back to the brick building so hard and fast all she could do was whimper.

Finally, I had the opportunity to bring my mouth to her throat, sucking and biting just enough to leave small marks. I slid lower and she clutched my hair while I brushed my lips along her cleavage, my hands wandering to her delicious tits. The alleyway was dim, out of the shine of the streetlamps, but I could hear people walking past, talking and laughing, completely unaware of the tryst taking place just inches away.

Fucking hot.

I took fistfuls of her thick hair, and inhaling deeply, drank in this mind-blowing pretty girl. As I fingered her curls, I felt like silk was pouring through my hands. My lips found their way back to hers, now swollen from my roughness, and they parted lightly to allow me to explore. Hers flicked back, tasting me and teasing me, until I thought I would shoot my load right there in the alley.

I backed her up to ensure we were completely in the shadows, our feet crunching on the gravelly ground, surely giving us away if anyone cared to find us. Which they didn't. And if they had, I would have sent them running so fast, they wouldn't know what hit them.

"How're you doing, gorgeous?" I asked.

"Mmmm," she murmured. "Your kisses are amazing."

Now that was just the kind of thing I liked to hear.

I reached for the button on her jeans, but before I opened them, I paused.

"You good with this?" I asked.

In the dim light, I could make out her nodding. "Yeah," she breathed, her lips planting butterfly-soft kisses in the crook of my neck.

I had her pants open and pushed below the cheeks of her ass in about a second flat, that was how bad I wanted to taste the rest of her. And I was sure in for a treat. I crouched 'til I was eye level with the pretty V between her legs, and before I could even bury my face in there, I experienced her excitement. Fuck, that was all I needed.

With her legs trapped together by the blue jeans circling the top of her thighs, her pussy was clamped shut. I wanted to get to the goods, but I was in no rush. When I moved my tongue to tickle the top of her slit, I found she was completely shaved. Goddamn. This woman was going to be mine if I had anything to say about it.

My tongue flicked between her pretty pussy lips. I opened her just enough to let her clit pop out into the night air. I was aching to dive in. But I didn't. Licking one of my thumbs, I rubbed it over her clit. She gasped, and when I looked up, her head was lolled back against the brick, her eyes half closed. She pressed her hands back against the rough wall to keep her balance.

"Damn, you smell good. And I know you're gonna taste better," I told her.

15

GARNET

God, the lumpy brick behind me, grinding into my back, was almost excruciating, but Win's tongue—first on my lips and then on my pussy—countered the abrasive, unyielding wall that held me up. The contrast was delicious and searing, a combination of pleasure and pain that left me so dizzy with need, I was afraid I might start to cry.

And shit, I barely knew this guy.

But something about him felt safe. Secure. From the first moment he confronted me about snooping around Grandpa's property, I'd had a feeling he was a man who knew his strength and made sure to protect the ones he loved. And of course, it didn't hurt that he was one gorgeous outdoorsman, with his lined, tanned face and unkempt bedhead hair.

And I loved that he checked in with me and didn't assume he could take whatever liberties he wanted, even if I was nothing more than a puddle of mush under his hands. And at that very moment, his tongue was flicking in and out of the top of my pussy lips, tormenting my clit, which was engorged and hungry for more. My legs were trapped tightly together since my jeans had been pushed down just below my ass, which kept Win's somewhat. But he managed to keep busy with the small bit of me he did have.

I dragged my fingers through his mop of hair, kneading and pulling until he moaned, jerking his head back away from my gripping fists. His gaze met mine, and he yanked my jeans down my thighs, past my knees, and to my ankles. He helped me step out of one leg after pulling off my boots, leaving me open myself as much or little as I wanted.

But of course, I wanted to give him everything.

I propped my free foot on an upside down flowerpot and offered myself. If I didn't know better, I could swear he was trying to smell me, which I thought was odd until I realized the effect it had on him. He took a deep inhale with his eyes closed and then with his thumbs, gently pried my lips apart. The cool night air hit my open pussy, dripping my creamy juice onto the ground below. He hooked a finger through it and brought it to his mouth. With his gaze locked on mine, he tasted me with a smile.

"God, you taste great. Delicious, darlin'."

Thank god I had the wall behind me because otherwise I'd be lying prone, unable to do much besides breathe, and of course, let Win play with my tortured pussy. What more could a girl want?

Shit. There were voices getting closer, and then I realized they were coming up the alley. But just before the people—I couldn't be sure how many of them there were—saw us, they pulled open a door and piled inside, oblivious to Win and me and the fun we were having.

If that wasn't enough to send me over the deep end, I was suddenly brazen like I'd never been before. I opened my legs even further to invite Win's attentions and thrust my hips in his face. I'd never felt so slutty, and I loved it.

"You like my taste, baby?" I asked as he buried his tongue in my slit for a long stroke from ass to clit.

"God, yeah. Fucking awesome," he murmured, not breaking his stride.

The sensation of his tongue running from front to back between my legs made me tremble. He must have noticed, because he gripped my thighs with his huge hands and steadied me. And of course, to push me further open.

"Darlin', I want you to come for me. Come in my mouth."

I didn't need much more encouragement than that. My hands flew up to my breasts where, through my blouse, I pinched and pulled my hard nipples. That, combined with the rough texture of the wall and silky feel of his tongue, brought me to my edge.

My entire body began to shudder, and my breath came in gasps. Fortunately, Win had a good grip on me because otherwise there was no way I could remain upright while he continued tormenting me with his mouth. As I got closer, he focused solely on my clit, creating a tight suction that left my whole pussy throbbing.

That was it.

I screamed, right there in the alley, and came, right there in Win's face. He lapped up my juices like it was the best thing he'd ever had, neither of us caring any longer who might see or hear us. He stood just in time to catch me as I went toppling, his mouth pressed against mine so I could taste what he just had.

"So good, darlin'...so good," he murmured in between licking and nibbling my bottom lip.

When I was steady again, he bent to pull my jeans back up.

"Wow," I said.

I had a feeling I would sleep well that night.

"You wore me out," I said, laughing.

"Okay then, lady. Let me get you home."

I WAS AWAKENED BY MATTY. Again.

"Yo, bitch. What's up with the guys? Find a hubby yet?" He cackled wickedly.

Sometimes he annoyed the living shit out of me.

"You woke me up, Matty. Why do you do that?" I asked.

"Because," he explained, "if I have to suffer by going to work at normal hours in the morning, then so should my best friend. Take it as a compliment!"

"I don't see it as a compliment..."

"So. Which ones have you gone out with? And most importantly, which one has the biggest dick?"

"Oh, Matty. You're such a jerk." I pushed myself up in bed, my room still fairly dark thanks to blackout shades. I took a sip from the glass of water on my nightstand.

"Well?" he asked.

"Calm down. I've been out with three of them. And it looks like there is a fourth—a friend of one of theirs."

"So..." he prodded.

"So far, we have Nat, Linc, and Win."

"Ohmygod. *Hot* names—"

"Matty, are you gonna let me talk?"

Silence.

"Nat took me out on a sailboat we spent the night on. He's smart...and funny. And a great lover, I might add."

I could practically hear Matty biting his tongue, trying not to interrupt. He eventually would, though. He always did.

"Then, there was Linc, who owns a gym. Super buff. We played right there in his office, overlooking the basketball court. And last night was Win, the groundskeeper at Grandpa's property. We messed around in the alley next to the Zeitgeist bar and oh my god, was he amazing."

He waited a minute to make sure I was through talking.

"You. Little. Slutbag. I love it! You're finally becoming the wild woman I always knew you would," he said.

"You mean I'm becoming like you, don't you? Well, I'm not. I'm testing these guys out to see which I might be able to get married to."

"Yeah, yeah. Enjoy the ride, girl. Anyway, what do they say when you tell them you might inherit millions?" he asked.

"I'm not telling them that. Are you crazy? First, I have to find out whether they like *me* for me."

"Right. Makes sense. So when are you gonna choose?"

"I don't know. I have one more guy to go out with."

"Wow. When it rains it pours. Girl, you're about to have men *and* money. I think I hate you."

"Well, don't hate me yet. Because as of now, I have neither."

But god, I hoped that would change.

16

BROSE

Win must have talked me up because Garnet seemed happy to hear from me when I'd called. Damn, he was a good friend, always doing me a solid. A lot of people would think it was crazy to do what we do. Hell, it *was* crazy. But sharing a woman worked for us, and when we found the right one, it worked for her just as well. He was busy with Cordy's property, and I was working insane hours at the restaurant, so neither of us had what it took to be a full-time boyfriend. Between the two of us, we managed to make our women pretty damn happy. At least, that's what they told us.

So when Garnet agreed to go out with me, I felt like I'd won the lottery. She was smoking hot with those long waves and nice, round behind. When she walked into North by Northwest wearing a swingy little skirt, my cock sprang into action. I had a vision of walking down the street behind her with just enough wind blowing up the back of her skirt, leaving me a delicious view of her ass cheeks. Of course, framed by a pretty lace thong of some sort. God, I loved a woman's ass in a thong.

But I was getting ahead of myself.

I'd grabbed a seat at the restaurant's bar for a quick drink before she joined me. The place was pretty much closed for the night, with just a couple tables left to finish coffee and pay the bill. We didn't like to rush people out —it was a shitty way to treat folks who'd just dropped a boatload of money. Plus, it gave the head chef and me the chance to come out, say hello, and thank them for coming by. That was one of the most important roles of being a chef, welcoming diners. It made them feel real special.

"Brose, hi!"

She was all smiles. I loved that.

"Well, look at you," I said, trying not to drool. I didn't want to be *that* sort of guy. At least not yet.

"You don't look too bad yourself with those cool duds you've got there," she said.

I looked over my chef's jacket. "I managed to keep myself pretty clean today. No major spillage."

"Well done."

She was eyeing the bar, probably comparing it to the place where she worked. "Can I get you a drink?" I asked her.

"Oh, that'd be great. I bet you guys have the good stuff here. Unlike Drive By."

"Hey, there's a time for everything. Sometimes a fancy

place like this is called for, and sometimes a down-home place like Drive By is just what the doctor ordered."

I called the bartender over to get Garnet something bubbly and pink, and I got a refill on my Jamesons. Garnet turned to face me on her barstool and held her glass up as a toast. She also gave me a peek at her long, long legs, which ended in those little high-heeled boots all the girls were wearing.

"Here's to making new friends," she said with that crooked little smile that just about killed me.

"Cheers to that, goddammit," I said.

Christ, I wanted to kiss her.

"So Brose, how long have you been here as sous chef?" She looked truly interested, unlike some women I dated who just wanted to know if I was making bank yet.

I took a swig on my whiskey. "Four years. Started as a line cook and moved up pretty quickly. The head chef yells a lot, but that means he likes you." I laughed, shaking my head. The restaurant world was a funny one, no doubt about it.

"Are you hoping to be head chef someday?" she asked.

"Not sure. My real dream is to open my own place. But that takes a boatload of money. And time. And business skills that I don't have."

"There's always something in the way of the dream, huh? Did you always want to cook?"

As she was looking around, checking out the restaurant, I was able to stare at her without being a creep. She wore some sort of crisscross sleeveless top that showed just enough cleavage and showcased her silky skin. I followed her arms down to her fingers, which were long, thin, and delicate. Hard to believe she shilled cheap beer all day long.

"Hell, yes. Ever since I could reach the stove, I've been cooking. My mom taught me a lot about the southern dishes she was raised with. When I get the chance to develop a recipe, I take what I learned from her as a starting point and kind of update it with today's trends."

Her eyes widened. "Are you gonna cook for me tonight?" she asked.

"Heck yeah. The last of the diners are just about gone, and Chef said I could have the run of the place. I picked up some groceries. I gotta be honest with you, however."

Trepidation washed over her face. "What?"

"I'm putting you to work. You'll be my assistant."

She threw her head back and laughed. "Fair enough! Let's go."

I unpacked the steelhead trout I'd picked up from the fishmonger and got Garnet to work chopping vegetables. I had to see if she was competent in the kitchen. I didn't mind teaching, but if she had no interest in fine cuisine, that would be a problem for me. Just like Win would expect whatever woman he was dating to have some affinity with the great outdoors. She didn't have to hike the Himalayas, but if she couldn't get her hands dirty with a bit of gardening, all bets were off.

To my delight, she sliced and chopped like an old hand.

"Hey, you're doing great there," I told her.

"Actually," she said, looking at me with a smile, "I love to cook. It's such a treat to be in a giant kitchen like this with room to spread out and all the tools you need."

I knew exactly what she meant. "Agreed. I feel like a kid in a candy shop in this kitchen. The possibilities are endless."

That's why I loved cooking. I never ran out of ideas.

And I also had some ideas about what to do with my own little sous chef.

I bent across the prep table where Garnet was hard at work and reached for her with my lips. To my delight, she stopped what she was doing and tilted her face toward mine.

As soon as we touched, an electric jolt shot through me, leaving my toes fiery with tingling. I had to stamp my feet to make sure they were still there, all the while keeping my connection with some of the most delicious lips I'd ever tasted.

"Mmmm," she murmured.

I pulled back and licked my lips. I had to leave her wanting more.

She boldly gave me her crooked smile, as if she'd been anticipating my affection. Which was good. It meant she was open and interested.

Win had told me he'd a great date with her—that she was smart, ambitious, and sexy as hell. He also told me she hadn't balked at the idea of us sharing her. I hoped my time with her might seal the deal.

I walked around to the side of the table where she was prepping and stood behind her, one arm on either side. She was effectively trapped between me and her work, her delicious ass pressed against my growing erection. With a tilted head, she gave me her neck, which was soft as an angel and smelled even better.

I dragged my lips over her heated skin as she put down her knife and the vegetables to press harder against me. Looked like dinner might be a bit late.

17

GARNET

Good lord, Brose was one beautiful man with his smooth brown skin, shaved head, and curly eyelashes. And when he ran his lips up my neck, I had to put down the vegetables I was chopping. I didn't need a knife in my hand when I might possibly pass out.

I leaned onto the stainless table where I'd been working, and he pressed a huge cock against the crack of my butt. His hands moved from the table where he'd wedged me and began to stroke my bare arms. My skin pricked into goosebumps, and a throbbing built between my legs.

His fingers reached between mine, and he gripped them in a gentle embrace, rubbing his erection into me. His breath quickened.

He was as turned on as I was.

I dropped my head back and he showered the side of my face with light kisses until I turned enough that our lips could meet again. Eventually, I was fully facing him, still pressed against the prep table, but this time, with his hard-on grinding into my tummy.

He put his hands on either side of my face, and his gaze drilled into mine.

"Beautiful, just beautiful."

A heated blush washed over my face. Every girl loved a compliment, but why did it always feel so damn embarrassing?

Maybe because I felt like I didn't deserve it? Anyway, this was not the time to try to make sense of my insecurities.

Brose continued studying my face. "Win told you about our um, particular appetites?"

Ah-ha. I had been waiting for that.

"Yes. Yes, he did." I nodded slowly. I was still trying to figure out what it all meant, but I had to admit, I was intrigued. Of course, I'm not sure it moved me closer to my mission of finding a husband in what was now two weeks' time, but at least I had options.

Brose fisted my hair to bring me to him and ground his lips down on mine, fierce and primal, like a man starving for oxygen. I draped my hands around the back of his neck and let myself melt into him, running my fingers over his smooth, bald head, playing with the thick hoop rings dangling from each ear.

His hands wandered down my back, where he pulled me away from the table just enough to reach under my skirt for a fistful of ass in each hand. His huge mitts felt like fire on my sensitive skin, even more so when he kneaded so hard I nearly cried out. Thank goodness for the table behind me.

Before I knew it, he'd propped me up on it, the stainless steel icy against my skin and just as shocking as his heated hands had been. He lifted my butt enough to yank off my thong, leaving my sex against the cold table. I rocked back and forth to keep myself from sticking.

His fingers found my wet opening and slowly entered until they were buried to the knuckle. He made that *come here* gesture, putting the perfect pressure on my G-spot. My breathing began to come hard, and my moans echoed, filling the empty kitchen.

Grabbing his arm, I helped him piston my pussy faster and harder, gasping for air as he brought me to my edge. From my position seated on the edge of the table, I drew my knees up and placed my feet on the shelf below for leverage. Brose was finger-fucking me so hard that if I didn't find a way to hold on, I might have flown across the room.

"Fuck me," I mumbled, unable to form anything more coherent. "Please, Brose, give it to me..."

As my moans turned to screams, he opened his jeans and freed one of the most beautiful cocks I'd ever seen, long and smooth and brown. While he worked me through my orgasm, he stroked himself to his own, spurting beautifully against the top of my thigh.

"Fuck, fuck, fuck," he mumbled, leaning his forehead to mine.

We finished the dishes after an incredible meal and left the restaurant, hand in hand. While he locked up the doors to North by Northwest, I spotted a homeless man tucked into a doorway, watching the passersby.

"C'mon," I said to Brose. We darted through the late-night traffic toward the other side of the street.

"Here you go," I said to the homeless guy, handing him the leftovers Brose had let me take home.

The man looked up, first at me, then Brose. Slowly, he extended his hand to accept the food. He didn't say anything while he opened the small box, and after he looked inside, he looked back up at us, still silent. That was all the thanks we were going to get, and that was all the thanks we needed.

What a night. And it still wasn't over.

"That was really cool of you," Brose said with a smile as we walked to his car.

I shrugged. "It's not every day we can do something nice like that. It feels good, doesn't it?"

"It does. It really does."

He pulled up to my apartment less than ten minutes later and leaned across the front seat to kiss me.

"Are you coming in?" I asked.

He shook his head slowly. "I hope you don't mind, but I'd rather not. I have to be back at the restaurant early to accept a delivery. But," he said with a giant smile, "I will definitely take you up on that another time."

Huh. I don't think I'd ever had a guy turn down an invitation to my apartment. But then, I'd been doing a lot of things lately that I'd never done before.

Like mess around with three other guys.

"Win tells me you'd like to be a sommelier some day."

"It's true. I mean, it's really just a pipe dream. But a girl can aspire, can't she?" I laughed.

"I could introduce you to the sommelier at our restaurant. You know, just for networking and learning. That sort of thing."

My heart jumped at the thought. And god, he was gorgeous in the streetlight.

"Really? That would be incredible. I would love to talk to another one."

He leaned back on the headrest. "You know, if you play your cards right, and I open a restaurant someday, you might find yourself with the job of your dreams."

What?

This guy was definitely a keeper. Even if he didn't want to marry me. Which he probably wouldn't, considering he didn't even want to spend the night with me. But hey, I'd take what I could get.

"Good night, beautiful," he said with one last kiss.

"Good night, handsome." I ran my hand over his head and tweaked his earring. "Next time, I'll cook for you."

"It's a deal," he said with a laugh.

Since Matty had no qualms about waking me up early in the morning, I didn't feel too badly about calling him late at night, even if I knew he'd already be asleep. After one ring, I could hear him fumbling with his phone, probably looking for the speaker button so he could leave it on the nightstand and just speak as loudly as he always did.

"What?" he whined.

"Hi. Hope you don't mind—"

"I do mind, but tell me what's going on. Did you go out with the last guy?" He yawned loudly.

"I did. He was awesome. So sweet, good looking. And he cooked for me," I said.

"And…" I knew what he wanted to know, but tormenting him was so much fun.

"Oh, you know. We messed around a little," I teased.

"All right. Don't tell me a goddamn thing. See if I care." He went silent.

"Matty, what am I going to do? They're all great, and I have to choose someone like, *yesterday.*"

"Well, which one do you like the best?" he asked.

"I don't know."

"Which one kisses the best?"

"I don't know."

"Which one has the biggest dick?"

I had to laugh at that one. So typical Matty. "I don't know."

He sighed in frustration. "How the hell can you not know? What are they, all perfect?"

"No, no, of course not. They're not all perfect. But put together as a package, they are. They're totally perfect when you take them as a whole. I mean, there's nothing left to want."

Oh boy. I was in trouble.

There was rustling in the background. He was sitting up in bed. That meant he was serious.

"Okay. This is what you have to do. You like them all. You have to choose one. Get the key to Grandpa's house and ask them all to move in."

Now *that* made me burst out laughing.

"Oh Matty, you are too funny. I need to find one dude to marry, and you suggest I live with all of them. Okayyyy..."

"Garnet, now listen to me. This is the solution to your problem. If any of them say no, then they've self-eliminated. If they say yes, they're in the running. What do you have to lose, besides five million fucking dollars?"

Five million dollars was a lot to lose. 'Course it wasn't mine to lose, at least not yet anyway.

18

NAT

I'd finally heard it all.

I liked Garnet. A lot. She was great. Pretty, good sense of humor. Sexy.

But move into some goddamn mansion with a bunch of other guys so she could choose one of us? That was the stupidest idea I'd ever heard.

So I said *yes*.

I needed to shake things up in my life. I'd been working too hard for too long. There was nothing spontaneous left. I was turning into an accounting drone, just what I'd always dreaded. I did want to become partner in the firm, but c'mon—at what cost? I'd finally met someone cool thanks to my swimming buddy Jonesy, and...

Wait. Was this a fix-up? Jonesy, who threw a lot of business my way, was always bugging me about meeting a girl. He'd sent me to her under the guise of 'potential new client.' Which she sure as hell wasn't going to become, at least not from what I could tell.

Yeah, no.

Something was just not adding up. Why did she even have him as her a goddamn attorney, anyway?

But I was going with it. Not gonna analyze it to death. Shit, that's what I did every day at work. And it was sucking the life out of me.

Maybe the other guys would be cool. At the very least, I hoped they wouldn't be douchebags. I was still traveling a lot, so I wouldn't see a lot of them anyway.

So, I was giving it a shot. She'd convinced me to try it for a couple weeks. It sounded crazy as hell, but you know, *YOLO*.

"Nat! Nat, over here!" Garnet called from inside the freaking huge mansion that was going to be my home for a week or two. The place was stunning in a Downton Abbey sort of way, which I'd watched once on an airplane somewhere. It was situated on a point in Belvedere, across the bay from San Francisco, with the kind of views of the city that I didn't even know existed.

She rushed up to me, out of breath. And beautiful, of course.

"Nat! I'm so happy to see you." She planted a nice kiss on my cheek and grabbed my hand. "Follow me."

"You're the first here, so you get first pick of the bedrooms." She was clearly hoping I'd be happy with this unearned advantage. And I guess I was.

"Amazing house. So, what are the options?"

Actually, I really wanted to ask her where *her* room was, but I didn't want to come off as an ass. After all, I did hope to spend some time with her. Some quality time.

"Well, this is the second floor, and then there's another one up above. All the rooms have their own bathrooms. At least the ones I've seen."

She dropped her head back and laughed at the absurdity of a house with too many rooms to visit.

Garnet's phone rang, and she fished it out of her pocket.

"Oh, it's my mother. Huh." She looked at me and excused herself.

From around a corner, I heard her.

"Mom? Hi..." and then I didn't hear anything else I could clearly make out.

Not that I wanted to.

So I took the chance to poke around on my own. I dropped my duffel bags at the top of the stairs so I could wander unencumbered. She was right—each bedroom had its own bath, which made me extremely happy. I hated sharing bathrooms. I guess I'd been staying in hotels so long, I wasn't used to sharing much of anything. Each room was beautifully furnished with a huge bed, sitting area, walk-in closet, and dressing table. Whoever owned this house was one lucky—and rich—bastard.

Speaking of which, how Garnet came to inhabit this place was a total mystery to me. But again, I reminded myself, relax and go with it. Someone like her could be a good influence on me with her carefree approach to life.

I climbed the staircase to the third floor and found that each bedroom up there had a killer view across the bay of San Francisco. I figured I had to grab one of those rooms, even if I ended up being miles from Garnet. I'd make it work. I headed back down to gather my bags and stake my claim in a room with a huge balcony, when I overheard her still on the phone with her mother.

"Mom, I'm sorry, but this is not a good time to visit. I'm…um…very busy. Yeah, with work and um…everything. Mom, you never want to visit me. What's so urgent about coming now?"

I grabbed my bags and headed to my new room, not wanting to eavesdrop. I could certainly understand Garnet's not wanting her mom to come right now. She *was* busy, about to be juggling four guys who each wanted her. And whom she wanted in return, I supposed.

I began to empty my things into the dresser and armoire in my new room when I heard a sound at the door.

"Hey there. Sorry I had to abandon you. Looks like you found a place to call your own."

I looked around the room, which was, incredibly, nicer

than any of the five-star hotels I'd ever stayed in. She walked in and plopped on the edge of the bed.

"It's pretty awesome here. Should be a good time," I said.

She smoothed her hand over the comforter where she was sitting. "Yes, I really hope so. This is quite the experiment." She laughed like she was nervous.

"It is indeed. When will the other guys be here?"

She looked at her watch. "Soon, I think. Soon."

I sat down on the bed next to her. "So we have a bit of time alone, then?"

Her face brightened. "Yes, I think we do." She crossed the room to close my bedroom door and headed back to me.

"Why don't you lay back and let me take care of you?" she asked.

Shit. I wasn't going to argue.

I kicked my shoes and socks off and jumped onto the bed that would be mine. Damn, it was comfortable. Shame I'd have to get up every morning to go to work. I could have really dug my heels into a place like this.

As soon as I was on my back with my hands behind my head, Garnet straddled me with her long legs, her dress kicked up to her thighs. I placed my hands on her fleshy legs and enjoyed her silky skin as she brushed against my crotch. In about two seconds, I had the raging hard-on I'd been fighting all day, which I had to subdue every time I thought of her.

Her lips were on mine in a flash, and while I had to

admit I'd not known many women to take charge, her confidence just about sent me over the deep end.

While we kissed, she made quick work of the fly on my blue jeans. In moments, my hard cock was in her hands, where she began slow strokes from root to tip. I had to focus to avoid coming right there on her pretty dress.

Her gaze locked with mine while she stroked me up and down. I reached for her tits and through her clothing, pinched and pulled her nipples. Her eyes fluttered closed and through her dress and panties, she rocked on my leg. Her hair fell forward over her shoulders, and damn if she wasn't more beautiful than a freaking movie star.

She wrestled out of my grip, and her tongue was on me, first licking my precum and then circling the head of my cock. It was so goddamn good, and even better watching her fucking hot technique. She parted her lips wider, and my cock disappeared into her mouth as she devoured me, gagging only slightly on my length.

She went back to the head of my raging dick, circling me with a greedy hunger that made me feel like a million bucks. I mean, who wouldn't want to be desired like that?

Her cheeks hollowed as she sucked me, and in moments, I felt my cum flow from my balls up the length of my cock and into her mouth.

"Fuck, baby," was all I could manage.

Her gaze locked onto mine as she licked the last drops of cum from me, moaning like she was about to get off, herself. When she was done, she plopped down next to me on the bed, burrowing into my arms.

Just as I was dozing off, she sat up.

"Oh, that's the doorbell. I think this will be Linc. I hope you guys like each other. I really do." She jumped out of the bed and straightened her clothes and hair.

"C'mon. Time to meet one of your new housemates."

19

GARNET

I RAN DOWN THE STAIRS TO SEE WHO WAS AT THE DOOR, relishing the freaking hot session I'd just had with Nat. God, what a great guy he was. Maybe I should just choose him—or ask him to marry me, as it were—and put an end to the suspense that was my life.

But when I opened the door and saw the gorgeous Linc standing there, I reminded myself not to be hasty.

"Linc!" I screamed, throwing my arms around him.

"Beautiful," he said, planting his lips on mine. That is, until Nat cleared his throat behind us.

The moment of truth.

Linc jerked his head up, looking over my shoulder. For a moment, I held my breath.

But I needn't have worried, at least at that moment.

"Dude!" Linc said to Nat, wearing a big smile and extending his hand.

And Nat looked just as cordial.

"Hey, man. I'm Nat." He took a couple large steps toward Linc and then shook hands the way manly men did, with the slap on the back with the opposite hand.

It would almost be easier if there were animosity. I could make my choice. But it seemed like they weren't going to do that for me.

Linc looked around, his eyes bugging out.

"Jesus, would you look at this place? We really get to stay here for two weeks?" he said.

Nat answered before I could. "Yeah, can you believe it? This place is fucking awesome. Hey, I understand you own a gym and are a trainer. I'd love to get some tips from you on improving my workout."

Linc nodded, his face all enthusiasm. "Let's do it. I'll work you so hard, you won't know what hit you."

Nat laughed and clapped him on the back. Linc looked over at me.

"Just ask Garnet, I can be a hard ass when it comes to working out."

"He's not kidding," I said. "Just you wait."

I gestured toward the stairs. "Shall we choose your room?"

Linc nodded enthusiastically. "Yeah, sure. But I don't need anything fancy."

"Dude, there's nothing here that's *not* fancy," Nat offered.

"He's right," I said.

I watched the two of them head for the stairs, figuring I'd let them do their thing. They were so hot I felt a little twinge between my legs as I imagined getting both of them into my bed. I'd not thought that far ahead, but now that it dawned on me, it seemed a possible bonus of our unique arrangement.

Would the guys feel like rivals? Or partners in crime? And would I be the lover they'd never forget? Or hate?

So many questions.

"Hey guys! Where'd you go?" I called, dashing up the stairs after giving them some time to decide whether or not they were going to get along.

"Up here," a distant voice said.

Following their voices, I realized they'd made it to the third floor.

Linc had taken a room down the hall from Nat, one with equally impressive views of the San Francisco skyline.

"Wow," I said, looking around Linc's newly-chosen room. "This one's just as amazing as the others."

After he finished unpacking, he sat on the end of the bed and stretched his hands out toward me. I hustled over for his warm embrace. He just felt so damn safe. Not to mention, big and strong.

"Baby, this is awesome."

"Are you sure? You're okay with this?" I asked.

"Nat seems cool. I'm looking forward to meeting the other guys."

My nervousness over our arrangement went down a couple notches.

But would it last?

"Mr. Jones, hi, it's Garnet."

Since Grandpa's attorney had made it possible for me to use the house, I felt compelled to check in.

"Garnet! If it isn't my most interesting client."

"I don't know that I'm interesting. I just think my situation is."

He laughed. "Well put. It's not every day an attorney administers an estate that stipulates marriage in thirty days or the deal is off."

Glad he thought it was funny.

Me, not so much.

But I had to say, the guys I'd met were pretty damn awesome, even though it didn't mean my problem was solved. Funny how things worked. Maybe I'd end up alone, and as broke as ever, but I'd have one hell of a story to tell.

"So Mr. Jones, I know I only have two weeks left but

I'm feeling like one of the four guys moving into the house might work out."

"I'm glad to hear that, Garnet. I really want this to work out for you. I know Mr. Cordy wanted his estate left to someone worthy."

"It's so odd that he did choose me. I mean, like I've told you, he and I barely ever spoke. It's just the strangest thing."

"Life works in mysterious ways."

"I guess. So two of the guys just moved in, and we're waiting on the others. I'll keep you posted."

"Sounds good. And give me a call if you need anything."

Ugh. I needed lots of things, but nothing an attorney could help me with.

"C'MON GUYS. Let's get going!" I called up the stairs.

To think men complained about getting women out the door.

"Hey babe, on the way," Nat hollered.

He and Linc, both dressed for the gym, came down the stairs together, talking about football scores. Or was it basketball scores?

It was all the same to me.

"And don't you look cute, my little gym rat-esse," Linc laughed.

He looked at Nat. "Whaddya think of our fine friend here?"

Nat turned his gaze to me, and the way he looked me up and down made my legs wobble and nipples stand at attention—a reaction not lost on either guy. Jesus, I didn't know how I would survive this, much less when the other two guys moved in.

Nat licked his lips, his gaze boring into me so directly, I wanted to tear my clothes off and jump on him.

Or both of them.

But that wasn't part of the deal. Was it?

"Okay, let's go, you two horn dogs."

Linc drove us across the bridge into San Francisco in his Jeep. Nat had hopped in the front with him, and they continued their sports talk like they'd been friends for years. I felt left out until I realized how damn lucky I was they were hitting it off.

"Okay, young lady, get ready to sweat," Linc said, opening the back door of the car for me.

We headed inside, the guys still gabbing about lifting weights.

"Hey," Linc said, "let's run up to my office first."

We followed him, passing his brother, who was headed to a session with one of his clients.

Linc closed the office door behind us. And then he locked it. I turned to see both men smiling at me.

How come I suddenly felt like prey?

"Garnet."

My name was a growl from Nat's lips, pouring over me, leaving me shaky. God, what had I gotten myself into?

I swallowed, looking from Nat to Linc and back. I had the distinct feeling they'd planned this. I'd never been with two guys at once. Had they had threesomes?

But now was not the time to interrogate anyone. No, now was the time to have fun. In two weeks, it would all be over. I could be with someone new.

Or I could be alone.

As they stared me down, they were such a sight to behold—Nat with his preppy, chiseled looks, and Linc with his short ponytail and facial scruff—each of them bringing their own unique brand of sexy to the table. But there was something about the two of them together, as if they were feeding off one another. Their combined sensuality was way more intense than merely taking each's lust and adding it together—it was as if two plus two equaled way more than four.

How does that even happen?

My reverie was interrupted by a harsh knock on the office door. I guessed Jack was done with his client meeting and had come back to his desk, which meant whatever Nat and Linc had planned for me would be put off 'til later.

But when I looked at the guys, they were both wearing smiles.

What the hell was going on?

"Baby, can you grab the door?" Linc asked, arms crossed in front.

Um. Okay.

I crossed the room, fighting to keep myself steady and at least *appearing* to be under control.

I threw the latch on the door and yanked it open, annoyed by all the weirdness.

Shit.

Who stood there, other than *Win*?

20

WIN

When I'd gotten word about the invite to move into the 'Big House,' as I'd called it when Cordy was alive, I was all about giving it a go. Why the hell not? The other guys sounded cool. In fact, one of them, Nat, had tracked me down with a plan to surprise Garnet at Linc's gym. I was all over that shit.

But poor Garnet. When she opened the door to Linc's office and I stood there as her surprise, she looked like she might have a freaking heart attack. We guys had meant to show her some fun, make her feel special. Instead, she looked like she'd been ambushed. I guess it was a bit much to take in.

"Hey darlin'," I said, putting my hands on either side of her face and kissing her temple. Under the circumstances, I wanted to proceed carefully. Glancing at the other guys, I could tell they were thinking the same.

"Win," she said, looking from me to the others.

"What…what are you doing here? I was going to introduce you to the guys when you moved in."

Her face was white as a ghost. Now I felt shitty.

Nat stepped forward. "Garnet, when you told me about the other guys moving in, Linc and I thought we'd surprise you. So we tracked down Win. Brose had to work, but Win agreed to meet us here. We thought this would make you happy."

Her expression softened, and she let out a long breath.

"Gosh. I'm sorry, guys. This is a lot for all of us to take in, and I guess I was just taken aback." She smiled and even released a small laugh. She settled on the edge of one of the desks and shook her head.

"I'm glad you're all here. It means a lot that you went out of your way for me."

Goddamn, she was beautiful. And she looked cute as hell in her gym clothes—little black leggings and some sort of tank top that showed off her delicious tits. Thank god I was wearing an untucked T-shirt that covered my growing cock.

As if on cue, Linc walked around the side of the desk where Garnet had perched and began gently rubbing her shoulders. He leaned down and kissed the side of her neck.

"Baby," he whispered. "Relax. Close your eyes and relax."

She took a deep breath. Nat crossed the room and re-locked the office door with a *click*.

When I was invited to join the group in Cordy's house,

Garnet had explained she liked a few different guys, and she thought moving us all in would be a great way to get to know us better.

I knew Brose and I would be down with an arrangement like that. Shit, we'd pretty much been through it before. It had worked out great until Esme had to return to France. I knew we'd both always love her—but everything has its season.

It had been a good set-up for everyone. Neither of us had much in the way of jealousy issues, and together, we were a better boyfriend than we'd each be on our own. We were all really happy, and I'd often wondered since if another arrangement like that might come our way. And what a sweet deal, moving into the mansion, but also keeping my apartment over the garage. I could always escape if I needed time to myself. Talk about perfection.

But nothing was a done deal yet. The final decision was up to Garnet. The beautiful Garnet.

"Oooh, that's nice," she purred as Linc worked her shoulders. As she relaxed, he laid her back on the desk, lifting her top just enough to kiss her belly. Her legs automatically parted to give him better access, and I knew we were on our way.

Her hands floated up to her tits and brushed over them lightly, leaving rock-hard nipples in their wake. Damn if that didn't leave me with a throbbing hard-on and a hunger unlike anything I'd felt in a long, long time. In fact, every molecule in my body wanted to tear off her workout tights and run my tongue up and down her slit 'til she creamed both my face and the desk she was lying on. I wanted to know how she'd look when she felt my thick cock deep between her legs as she came all over me and my balls.

But there would be time for that soon.

And that wasn't all I wanted. What would she look like in the morning when she woke up? What made her laugh? What was her favorite band? I knew nothing about her and yet, was so drawn to her.

Like I said, I'd known we'd be together, one way or the other, from the moment I met her.

Linc continued laying kisses on her belly, working his way up to her tits, while Nat was at the other end of the desk at her head, sprinkling kisses on her forehead, cheeks, and sides of her neck. She smiled slightly and squirmed every now and then as if to ask for more.

Linc pushed up her shirt to free her gorgeous tits, and then moved back to the area between her legs covered by nothing but stretchy workout fabric. The shape of her pussy was outlined by her tights, and as Linc stroked it with his fingers, her lips became even more prominent. She smelled so good, all womanly and turned on.

As Nat moved to her mouth, and Linc remained between her legs, I dove into her luscious breasts, licking, sucking, and nibbling until she moaned. I looked up to see Nat had pulled his dick out and was teasing her mouth with it. My own hand found mine and had to stroke it through my jeans to keep myself in line.

But hell, if Nat was whipping his out, I wasn't keeping

mine in my pants. In no time, I jumped up on the desk, straddled Garnet, and began to rub my cock between her pretty tits. She helped by pushing them together.

Holy shit, I could fall in love with this woman.

Linc was behind me, working his magic on her pussy, and even with her mouth full of Nat's erection, she still managed to moan.

Cum flowed from my balls to the root of my cock. With my hands over Garnet's, I tightened the friction on my cock between her tits. I drove between them with a fury and pinched her nipples until she winced. As my explosion started, I released her tits and directed my stream all over her chest, neck, and chin. I kept pumping 'til I was dry, grinding my balls against her.

I crawled off her in time to see Nat spurt in her mouth and to watch her try to take it all down her throat.

"Good girl. Such a good girl."

21

GARNET

Holy. Fucking. Shit.

I'd never been with two guys before, never mind three, but there I was, getting my group sex cherry popped in Linc's gym like people did that every day.

Maybe they did do that every day, and I was just out of the loop. It was entirely possible.

My breasts were on fire, thanks to Win's attentions, and as Nat exploded into my mouth, I rubbed Win's cum over every part of my body that I could reach. I could have had it in my eyeballs and wouldn't have cared at that point.

That left Linc, who, when I looked up after devouring Nat's cock, had fetched a condom from somewhere and was rolling it down over his own. Both the other guys stepped aside to watch the show, but before Linc did anything, his gaze locked with mine.

"You good, baby?" he asked.

"Yes…yes…give it to me. Please," I begged.

He leaned close to my ear. "You're fucking amazing, Garnet."

His crown was pressed against my opening, but before he entered, he looked at the guys. "Either one of you assholes want to help me out here?"

Nat and Win moved toward the end of the desk, each taking ahold of one of my legs so they could spread me open—wide open. With all eyes on me, I felt shy for a moment, but when I saw their caring faces, it passed.

If only Brose could be there.

Linc reached one hand under my chin and turned my head to watch. With his gaze still locked on mine, he rubbed his cock up and down my slick pussy, opening my lips so they could all see me. I reached down to touch my clit and found myself so on fire with lust, I nearly exploded right there. But before I could, someone moved my hand away. They were gonna make me work for it.

So I reached for my tits and pulled hard on my nipples, driving a shocking sensation straight past my belly button to my tormented core.

"Open that pretty pussy for me guys," Linc growled. Fingers landed on either side of my opening, gently pulling my lips apart to leave me ready. But before Linc entered me, he drove a finger inside, pulled it out, and thrust it into his mouth.

"Fucking A, baby, you taste good."

Slowly, slowly, I was opened by Linc's giant cock as he eased his bulging crown inside me.

"Oh god, Linc. It's so big…"

"Take it, baby…you can take it…take my cock until my balls bounce off you."

He drove all the way inside me until I shrieked with the sensation of being so full. Nat and Win pushed my legs back as far as they could go, each with a hand on their own cocks, which were, to my amazement, already hard again.

Linc was so deep inside, I felt him in every nerve. He slowly pulled out, leaving me whimpering, and filled me up again as our bodies came together. I'd never felt so wide open, like I was *giving* myself not only to Linc, but also to the other guys.

I grasped the hands that Nat and Win had on my legs, and I swear to god, it really felt like we were all fucking together. The intensity made the room spin as I was fucked with deep, purposeful strokes until the dirty pleasure of being with three men began to swallow me. Linc's cock stretched me again and again as he made me his. Each of the guys in his own way was making me *his*.

Someone's hand, I couldn't be sure whose, slid below my bum and settled on my ass. Holy shit, I'd never really been interested in doing anything back there, but in my heightened state, I probably would have said yes to anything.

The finger probing me back there took advantage of my slipperiness and pressed until I opened enough for it to venture just inside. It circled around, relaxing my tight ring, and driving me wild. I hadn't known that sort of play could feel so great, and tiny explosions tunneled through my every pore. I reached one of my hands to my clit and rubbed furiously. I needed my orgasm and I needed it now.

With a finger in my ass plunging deeper and deeper, and Linc hitting every spot inside me, the room spun, and I wasn't entirely conscious anymore. All I could do was mumble, whimper, and occasionally scream.

Someone's fingers pressed into my clit. They might have been mine, or one of the guys, I was no longer sure. It didn't matter. A masculine growl filled my ears, and my world shattered. I screamed as I came for these lovely men.

I was hardly aware of being scooped up by several arms and moved to something soft and cushiony. Lips fell on mine, I had no idea whose, and I found myself held by deep and powerful arms.

"Garnet? You okay?" a voice asked me.

I was coming back into the room, but my legs shook like they'd never stop. When my vision cleared, three devastatingly handsome men peered down on me with concern.

"Whoa," I said. "What time is it? I need to get to work."

Nat raised his hands to the *stop* position. "Hold on, hold on. We called the bar. Tom agreed to cover for you."

I looked from one face to the next in disbelief. "You can't do that. I need to work. I have bills to pay." I struggled to get up and push past them.

"Guys, you can't ask my coworker to cover for me. It's not fair to him."

"It's okay," Win said. "He offered. Said you can pay him back another time. He's expecting it to be a slow night, anyway."

Geez. I guessed this was what one might call teamwork.

I took a deep breath. "What did I do to deserve you? All three of you?" I asked.

"You're incredible. That's all," Linc said softly.

"Clearly no one has ever told you just how great you are, and that you deserve all the happiness there is."

My heart flipped, and in the next second, was seized by a crippling anxiety.

I was going to have to choose one guy to marry to get Cordy's estate. How in god's name was I supposed to do that?

22

BROSE

I FINALLY HAD A FEW HOURS OFF WORK TO MOVE INTO THE mansion Win had maintained all these years. I'd been inside many a time, invited for beers by the late Cordy, but never in my wildest dreams entertained spending one night there, never mind two weeks. I had to hand it to Win. The dude hooked my ass *up*.

First with a beautiful woman, then a freaking mansion.

True, I had no idea what might come of our funky two-week arrangement, but what the hell. Win had told me the other guys were cool, and that they'd already had a nice little group sesh with Garnet that left smiles all around.

Of course, he offered no details. Gentlemen didn't do that. But he didn't need to. I could tell from the look on his face, the guys had given our girl the time of her life. And to think we were all just getting started.

Christ. Did I just say *our girl*? I was getting ahead of my bad self, wasn't I?

Arriving at the mansion, I rang the doorbell. Although I'd be living in the place, I wasn't sure if I should just waltz in from the get-go.

"Dude!" Win hollered as he pulled the door open. He embraced me with a bear hug, even though we'd seen each other just a few days ago.

He seemed pretty goddamn happy, I had to say.

"Brose, come on over and meet the other guys."

I followed him from the foyer, past what had once been Cordy's office, to a game room outfitted with (of course) a pool table, but also a poker table, several wide screen TVs and reclining chairs, dartboards, and a couple vintage pinball games. That bastard Cordy had lived well.

"Brose, meet Linc and Nat." Two guys holding pool cues approached me, hands outstretched.

"Welcome aboard, Brose," Nat said.

"Thanks, thanks so much."

"Can I get you a drink?" Linc asked. There were glasses of brown liquor on the rocks being enjoyed all around. I was certainly ready for one of those.

"Cheers. Here's to the good life. And may Cordy rest in peace," Win said.

A round of *to Cordy* filled the room, and I took a long draw on what I guessed was Jameson's fine whiskey.

"Dude, you gotta pick a bedroom," Win said. The other guys nodded.

"You're the last in, but every room is great so you're not gonna be wanting for anything," Linc offered.

"Cool. Show me the way?" I said to Win, grabbing my bag.

I followed my friend through the house. "Christ, I forgot how awesome this kitchen was. I'm gonna do some cooking in this baby."

Win's face brightened. "We'll be forever in your debt if you hook us up with some good grub."

"Oh, I plan to. We'll be eating well. When I'm here, and not at work, that is," I added.

We headed up a massive staircase, where Win stopped.

"All us guys have chosen rooms on the third floor, and Garnet's is on the second. You want to be upstairs with all of us?" he asked.

"Sure. I don't want to buck the trend. Let's go."

Christ, I'd never been up to the third floor, because well, why would I have? And I had no idea it was so deluxe. Every room had a massive four-poster bed, a sitting area, and its own bathroom, which I was really psyched about. I had a feeling all us guys would get along great, but that didn't mean I wanted to share a pisser with any of them.

I chose a room at the end of the hall that seemed like it would be quiet and out of the way. Perfect for private time with Garnet, whenever that might occur. Speaking of which.

"Where's our girl?"

Win guffawed. "Listen to you! *Our* girl. Christ, dude, aren't you jumping the gun a bit?"

Jerk. "Hey, laugh all you want. I believe in the power of positive thinking. And I'm thinking positively about that babe and her nice fleshy ass."

"Did someone just say something about my nice fleshy ass?"

We whipped around.

Busted.

There stood the beautiful Garnet in the doorway wearing a long red robe.

But I didn't care if I were busted. If she didn't know now that I loved her ass, she'd be finding out soon enough.

"Gorgeous!" I said, and she came running into my arms. Of course, I took the opportunity during our embrace to grab her behind.

Talk about making a guy feel good. No, great.

I planted a big one on her luscious lips.

"I'm so glad you're here," she said with a huge grin. "Now we are together like one, big happy family."

I plopped down on the edge of the bed. "An unconventional family."

"But still a family," she said, clasping my hand. And damn if that didn't cause my dick to jump around in my pants. All I could think about was ripping that robe off her and spreading her creamy thighs…

She was so goddamn captivating, and perhaps the best

part about her was that she had no freaking idea how awesome she was. Gorgeous, smart, ambitious, and kind—I'd loved how she'd given her leftovers to that homeless guy after our date at North by Northwest.

The bedroom door closed and Win slowly made his way toward us with a sly smile. Maybe I really *was* going to have the opportunity to taste her delicious gifts. I was certainly banking on it, especially given how hard my cock was throbbing in my jeans.

Without giving her a second to think about being behind closed doors with Win and me, I pulled her tight to me, leaned in, and kissed her with everything I had. And it was better than I even remembered. Time stood still, and I got utterly and totally lost in her.

We eventually inched apart because one, we needed to breathe, and two, I couldn't hog her all to myself with my boy Win in the room. Her face was flushed from my surprise hit, but she was also awash in hungry need.

"Wow," she said, running a finger along her lips.

"I've been thinkin' about kissing you all day, beautiful."

Her face lit up with that fantastic, crooked smile, and before she could even move, Win approached her from behind, gently sliding her robe off her shoulders, leaving her wearing nothing but a silky pink thong. His hands slid over her bare shoulders and reached for her breasts. He cupped them from underneath while I reached for her nipples to gently pull. Her head lolled back, and she sighed like the sweet thing that she was.

But I wasn't done kissing her and pulled her to me again. This time, I was downright savage. I knew her lips would be red and sore later, and I didn't care.

Win laid her back on my bed, and while I continued kissing her, I pulled her thong panty off to expose her beautiful, shaved pussy. Her lips were puffy from her excitement, her clit poking out like it was ready to party.

Win and I were old hands at this threesome stuff, and while we never messed around with each other—it wasn't our thing—we did have a groove that worked for us as we enjoyed one woman. Garnet, now on her back, snuggled into me. I played with her tits and showered her with kisses while Win teased her clit with his roaming tongue.

She started to spread her legs to give Win better access, but he pressed them back together. He put one thigh on each side of hers to hold them together, to heighten the sensation of playing with her clit.

He pressed his tongue harder into her tight slit and she moaned, her head rocking back and forth on the bed. I pulled my cock out of my pants and had given it a couple strokes to relieve the pressure.

"Wait," Garnet said, sitting up. "I have an idea. Can you both take your clothes off, please?"

She didn't have to ask me twice.

"Win, can you come over here?" She gestured for him to move up toward the pillows.

"And Brose, can you lie down here on your back?" She pointed me toward the end of the bed.

I did what I was told.

And don't you know, our hot little mama placed her pussy right over my goddamn face, grinding it nice and good, just how I liked it, and grabbed Win's hard-on and devoured it in her pretty little mouth.

Our girl was pulling a train, and I was in goddamn heaven.

23

GARNET

I was so happy Brose had arrived. Now all my boys were together. Sure, I was having trepidation about the prospect of choosing only one out of the four—and I really had no idea how I would—but in the meantime, I planned to enjoy a short-lived life of a queen with a harem of princes who existed to serve her every beck and call.

Yeah, right.

But Brose and Win together? It was enough to make any girl feel she'd died and gone to heaven. I was in bed with two of the hottest guys I'd ever known, and they were all about pleasing me. 'Course I had every intention of returning the favor to both of them. These guys were hot alphas, taking what they wanted and leaving a trail of hunger in their wake.

While I ground into Brose's face, his hands held my hips, his fingers digging so hard into my ass I knew I'd have red marks later. Win, at my other end, held the root of his cock so I could focus on its swollen crown.

Brose slid out from under me and I heard the unrolling of a condom. Next, he pressed against me, doggy-style.

Win tilted my face up to his. "You ready, baby? You ready for some cock in your pussy?"

Since my mouth was full, I nodded yes, my body shivering from his dirty talk. Brose slowly slipped inside me, stretching me until I adjusted. I grimaced from the initial discomfort, but he moved slowly enough that my orgasm began to build right away. He groaned loudly, rocking his hips to get deeper, holding my ass cheeks for leverage.

His heavy balls bounced against my clit when he started to really fuck me, driving in and out, his big cock pounding until I thought I might pass out.

"Fuck, Win, she's squeezing my cock. She's squeezing—"

But he didn't finish whatever he was trying to say. Instead, he exploded with a roar that shook the room. I followed right behind him with my orgasm, pumping against him so hard, I'm surprised we didn't all fly right off the bed.

Win pulled his cock out of my mouth and spurted on my open mouth and tongue, screaming *"fuck, fuck, fuck..."*

Brose's stroking slowed, and he pulled out somewhere along the line getting rid of the condom.

The three of us fell under the bed's comforter to catch our breath, with me in the middle, of course.

Good god, what had I gotten myself into? There were four incredible men in my life—actually, in my house—and if I were honest about it, I was falling for each of them. A week or two ago, I wouldn't have believed it was even possible.

Time to talk to Matty.

"Yo, if it isn't my slutty best friend Garnet!" he cackled. "So how is it, living with four men? By the way, have I told you I *hate* you?"

"Oh, Matty, I think this may have been a mistake. I like them all. They're each so different from the other, in such amazing ways." I felt that familiar clutch in my chest, the one I got when I really thought about the situation I was in.

"I don't know what I'm going to do."

Matty let out a long breath. "You can't pick just one? I mean, c'mon, don't at least a couple of them do something that bugs the shit out of you? You know, like chew with his mouth open or interrupt all the time?"

It was a totally legit question, but the amazing thing was that no, none of them did much of anything to turn me off. That didn't mean they never would, but at that point in time, they each brought something different to the table that complemented the whole.

First there was Nat, my preppy accountant, trying to

get a life outside of work, who loved that I'd encouraged him to try something crazy.

Then, there was Linc, my muscular and hunky gym-owner who worked his ass off for the security he and his brother never had growing up. He quiet and sensitive, but an animal behind closed doors.

And Win, my rugged outdoorsman who was taken in by Cordy, the same man who wanted to help me, in his own crazy sort of way.

And last was Brose, my shaved head, pierced, and tattooed chef who had dreams as big as mine, and obstacles just as large to go along with them.

"Matty, what should I do?" I pleaded.

He waited for a moment before he spoke. "Here's what you need to do. Be honest."

"Huh? You mean tell them about the money?"

"Yup. Tell them the whole story. Whether you end up with one or none of them, if you really care about them, you can't deceive them like you already sort of are."

He was right. I knew he was right. I had to come clean and see where it got me. Like I'd said from the beginning, if I walked out of this with no man and no money, well, I wouldn't be any worse off than the day Grandpa's attorney tracked me down to tell me about the inheritance to begin with.

The funny thing was, I was pretty sure the guys felt the same way about me. Win and Brose were happy to share, so there was that. And Linc and Nat seemed completely at peace with it, too. How was it that jealousy wasn't tearing our happy little family apart?

Is this what Grandpa meant for me?

"I'm scared, Matty. Scared I might lose them all."

"You might. But if you're not honest with them, you definitely will."

I'D ARRANGED a dinner for all of us the next night, no easy feat with everyone's crazy work schedules. Nat got out of a business trip, Linc rescheduled one of his personal training clients, Win signed off early on the mansion's roofing job he was handling, and Brose got one of the other chefs to cover for him. I hadn't been at work much lately, but Tom had been happy to pick up the slack for me since he'd wanted to make some extra cash.

It was a treat to do something nice for the boys, so I planned a dinner of filet mignon with smashed brussels sprouts and other delectable sides. For dessert, I'd baked a Grand Marnier cheesecake, always a crowd pleaser. We had tons of great wine, thanks to the sommelier from North by Northwest and Brose.

I had everyone seated by eight p.m. and started serving. As we dove in, I raised my wine glass.

"I want to toast the four of you. These last few days have been the happiest of my life. I so appreciate your willingness to be open-minded and committed to the best for not only me but also the group itself. I never dreamed we'd all work this well together."

I swallowed the lump in my throat, and as the room filled with a chorus of *cheers*, I looked at each one of their beautiful faces as they helped themselves to the meal I'd thrown my heart and soul into preparing.

And wondered how many more of these there would be.

24

NAT

Not only was Garnet gorgeous and sexy, she could also cook like nobody's business. I needed to find a way to keep this woman in my life.

I'd just sliced into one of the best filet mignons I'd ever seen when she cleared her throat. I hoped it wasn't the speech I'd been dreading, the one where she sends each of us on our way. I mean, I knew it had to happen eventually, but I wasn't ready. Not yet, please.

"I have a few things to share with you, my handsome friends," she said.

Everyone looked up from their plates.

"There's a reason I had you all move into the mansion with me, and it's a bit different from the one I told you about in the beginning." She took a sip of her wine and nervously cleared her throat. She looked at each of us, one by one.

"I had a visit from an attorney three weeks ago now,

who came to tell me a man who'd been a regular at the Drive By Saloon where I work had died and left me his estate."

I sneaked a look at the other guys at the table. They were doing the same.

"The man who left me the money was named Bill Cordy and this was his house. Win and Brose knew him, but they didn't know about my inheritance," she continued.

I looked over at Win, who was white as a ghost.

Garnet continued, "The estate that was left to me is worth five million dollars…"

Holy shit. I set down my fork, like the other guys did. The attorney was Jonesy, and that's why he sent me to her to talk about managing her money.

"…and the only way I actually receive it is if I'm married within thirty days of the attorney notifying me."

"So what are you saying, Garnet?" I asked.

"The reason I asked everyone to move in was so I could choose one guy."

"And…?" Brose asked.

"And, I've found I have feelings for each of you. Strong and intensely powerful feelings for *four* men. And I have no idea what to do with that."

For a moment, no one made a sound.

Then Brose broke the silence. "You know how I feel about you, Garnet. Hell, you know how we all feel about you. It's scary for all of us."

"I'm fucking crazy about you," Linc said, looking around the table. "Brose is right. We all are."

Garnet's hand flew up to her mouth, and her eyes filled with tears. But there was no stopping them.

"I...I don't know what to do," she said through a shaking voice. "That money would change my life. It would change all our lives. Each of you has dreams, just like I do. I just don't know why Cordy stipulated that I had to be married." She buried her face in her hands. "It's so stupid...why did he do it..."

Win reached her first and drew her into his arms. She sobbed into his shoulder as he patted her hair. What a crazy fucking situation.

Garnet untangled herself from Win and stepped back from the table. "You know what, guys? I hate to ruin a great night, but I'm feeling like I need some time alone. I hope you'll excuse me. Please enjoy the rest of your dinner."

The sound of her high heels on the wooden floor got further away until her bedroom door slammed shut.

WHILE WE GUYS got along with each other, after that dinner, there was no denying the tension in the air. We all cared for Garnet and wanted the best for her. The thing was, the reality of which of us might end up with her was now on the table for all to see. One of us would be chosen, and the other three would... well, be shit out of luck. Our time together was not going to last forever.

That's why I was thrilled to get out of the house and go to work. Hell, I even scheduled the business trip I'd been postponing. I could leave at the end of the week and hopefully just forget about Garnet and the new friends I'd made. I needed to get back into the swing of things at work and focus on my career.

I went to work early the next day, just to get out of the house.

My desk phone rang, and I saw it was Jonesy, the attorney who'd introduced me to Garnet in the first place. I had a few choice words for him.

"Hey," I said.

"How are things with Garnet?" he asked.

What the hell did he mean by that? There was no way he'd know I'd been seeing her socially. Was there? And he couldn't know I was now aware of the five million dollars she stood to inherit. And I wasn't going to let on.

"Um, well, I met with her a couple weeks back just as you asked me to. She didn't seem ready yet to talk finances. But I'm sure she'll call me when she is."

"Uh huh. Right. Okay."

"Why do you ask? Do you know something different?" I couldn't be sure whether he was calling my bluff or not.

"No, just wondering where things were. I'll check in with you again next week, if you don't mind."

"Don't mind at all. Good talking to you."

Now that was an odd call. He'd sent me to Garnet

knowing she might be inheriting a pile of money. But he didn't tell me that, and he had no way of knowing whether or not I'd found out yet.

I didn't give a damn about the money. All I knew was I wanted Garnet in my life, hopefully as my girl, but if not, I'd accept her as my friend. And I really didn't want to lose the new buddies I had. They were great guys, and the cool thing was none of us got jealous when another was with Garnet. We all had our own lives and were busy as hell, so it was good to know someone else could take care of her when one of us couldn't.

An odd arrangement, sure. But strangely, at the same time it was also perfect.

25

GARNET

I FELT BAD FOR FLEEING THE DINNER TABLE WHEN I HAD A couple nights before, but I was suddenly overwhelmed with the fact that I held the future of four wonderful men in my hands. It was a weighty responsibility, and one I did not feel worthy of. I got back to my room and cried for the better part of an hour until I passed out, staying there for most of the next day until it was time to go to work. I slipped out of the house quietly and headed into the city.

It still baffled me that Grandpa required me to be married to inherit his estate. I mean, who pulled a requirement like that out of their ass, especially with only thirty days to carry it out? It just made no sense. In fact, it was freaking impossible. The first time the attorney came to see me, I should have told him to take a hike. The whole thing was a stupid waste of everyone's time.

On the other hand, I suppose I would have met the four guys, anyway, regardless of Grandpa's passing. Right?

Or could meeting them have been something orchestrated? Maybe it wasn't a coincidence at all.

I suppose if I had to, I could just ask Win to marry me. I mean, he'd been on Cordy's property for years, and god knew if anyone deserved to benefit from that, it was him. On the other hand, if I inherited the property, no matter who I ended up marrying, I could let Win stay. So I supposed I could marry Brose, because those two were sort of a package deal. But where would that leave Linc and Nat?

I couldn't bear the thought of hurting either of them. Linc, who was so sweet, and Nat, who was trying to break out of his corporate rut. They treated me like royalty, and I loved them for it.

Oh, shit. Did I just say love?

I meant liked. I liked them. A lot.

Plus, I'd never had sex like that before. Never, ever. And probably never would again.

My cell rang, and I saw it was Linc. I jumped to answer it, even though I probably shouldn't have.

"Hi," I said.

"Hey, beautiful. Do you have a few minutes?" he asked.

"Yeah. The bar doesn't open for another half hour."

"Can I come over to talk?"

"Of course," I said, my heart pounding. Was this the day he was going to tell me to go to hell? That he'd had enough drama, and besides wasn't about to share a woman on an ongoing basis?

I let him into the Drive By and locked the door so we

could talk in peace. There he stood, in all his hunky glory, his gym pants hugging his round ass, his hair scraped back into an unselfconscious ponytail.

He greeted me with one of his amazing, soft kisses. He was a fucking catch, no doubt about it. All thoughts of marrying Win, Brose, or Nat exited my mind as that familiar throb between my legs said *hello*.

"What brings you by?" I asked, continuing to unload beer bottles from their boxes into the cooler behind the bar. If I kept busy, he wouldn't see what a wreck I was.

He settled into a stool and watched me work. "Could I get some water?"

Maybe he was nervous?

I slid him a glass, and, suddenly parched, grabbed one for myself.

"So," he started, "the guys and I all met this morning."

What? They *met?* What *about?* Were they dumping me?

Shit. I knew it. I was going to end up with no one. No guy, no money, and no goddamn future.

Oh Grandpa, why did you have to mess with me to begin with? My life would have been fine without dangling five million dollars I couldn't possibly qualify for right in front of my face. I was happy in my generally mediocre existence. There was no need to push me into the miserable category.

I guess my face gave me away. "Wait, wait, Garnet. It's not like that. We're not ganging up on you," Linc said.

Damn, he really did read my mind. Another reason to love—I mean like—him.

I was moments from vomiting.

"We—all four of us—talked for a long time about our arrangement, and what you need to do to inherit Cordy's estate. You've been given the opportunity of a lifetime, and you can't let this slip through your fingers."

"I'm trying *not* to let it slip through my fingers, Linc, you know that. But maybe it's just not meant to be. I invited all four of you to move into the house so I could see which guy I was best suited to be with. And…I fell for all of you."

"Garnet, you have to choose. Pick one of us. We'll understand. We all want you to be happy, and we all want you to have the money, the estate, and to be able to realize your dreams. This is your chance to quit living hand to mouth, buried in debt with no way out."

His compassion was my undoing. I slammed the cooler door shut as my shoulders heaved and the tears began to flow—again. Really, I was getting tired of crying over this asinine situation. I didn't ask for it, and I didn't need it.

Linc came around the end of the bar, and I buried my face in his shoulder—so warm and comforting, smelling like—well, him. It was funny. I'd gotten to where I could almost identify all the guys by their scents, all wonderful and different in subtle but unique ways.

"Don't be sad, baby. It will work out. We won't let you down."

Well. That just made me cry harder. What had I done

to earn the affection of the four most amazing men I'd ever known? Surely, I didn't deserve a one of them.

"Baby." Linc hooked his finger under my chin and turned my face up toward his. With his broad thumb, he pushed the tears off my face and lowered his mouth to mine.

God, how could everything feel *almost* all right, so damn fast?

His lips brushed mine, sweeping away some, if not all, of my anxieties, and when I was ready to respond, I parted my lips so we could taste and explore. I pulled back to face him.

God, he was gorgeous. I mean, all the guys were, but Linc had this sexy, quiet power about him. It was irresistible.

He frowned. "You're worried."

"I…yeah, maybe. I mean, I guess so," I answered.

"Why?" he asked.

"I don't want to hurt anyone. You included."

"You're scared," he said. His eyes blazed into mine, his hands sliding toward my waist, leaving a trail of fire in their wake. "You're afraid of what you're feeling. It's not just the inheritance. We're all feeling it."

And who wouldn't be afraid of having feelings—strong, powerful feelings—for four men who not only knew each other but had also become friends.

"Garnet, I'm falling for you. We all are, for Christ's sake," he said huskily.

Shit. The second he said that, it was out there. Like

something big had just escaped, something big and dangerous, and it could not be recaptured. And he was right.

It scared the shit out of me. Four amazing, sexy as shit guys falling for *me*?

Scary, yeah. But it also sent a thrill through me that made my knees weak. The possibilities were…

Wait a minute. Choosing one would hurt the remaining three. I couldn't do it.

Out of the question.

I'd go back to my old life, just keeping my head above water.

No more cute guys. No more hot sex.

Linc continued, "It's funny, because the four of us are all pretty different. In most cases, we'd probably want different types of women. But it seems like *you* are our type."

Ugh. Why did he have to make this so hard?

He cupped my face with his hands. "So we all agreed that I'd talk to you."

"How'd they choose you?" I asked.

"They thought I'd be the calmest and coolest."

They had a point.

He took my hand and led me over to a booth, where he slid in next to me. He pulled me to him.

"We're all cool with you choosing one. You are more important to us than anything. There will be no jealousy, no resentment. And we'll always love you."

I shook my head. "I can't choose."

"You have to."

The gravity of what he was saying washed over me. It was so goddamn zero-sum. And so goddamn unfair. The naughty thrill of multiple lovers was coming to a screeching halt, just as I'd known it eventually would.

I just didn't know it would hurt so much.

He slid out of the booth and stood.

"You have to open the bar, and I have to get back to the gym. Meet us at the mansion tonight. We'll all be there, and we'll help you figure this thing out."

I watched him leave the Drive By, the sunlight flashed through the open door, and then disappeared, leaving me sitting in the dim bar alone.

"Matty," I said over my cell during the drive back to the mansion. "You busy?"

"Hey, sweetie. No, I'm not busy. I'm never busy. I don't believe in working hard. Actually, I don't believe in working at all, if one can help it."

It was true. He didn't.

"So, how are things with the guys? I'm still green with envy that you've got a fivesome going on."

"Well, it was awesome while it lasted."

He gasped. "What do you mean?"

"It's coming to a close, is what I mean. It's gone too far. And I can't play with people's lives like this."

I may not have been able to see him, but I knew he was giving me his best eye-roll. "C'mon. Don't you think you're being a bit dramatic? You sound like someone's going to die."

I felt a little bit like I might...

"We're meeting tonight to figure things out. But I've decided what I'm going to do," I said.

"Garnet, do not be foolish. I'm begging you. Think this through."

I *had* been thinking it through. That was the problem.

26

WIN

I poured myself a scotch while I waited for the rest of the guys and Garnet. I wasn't sure what was going to go down, and I was nervous as hell. Nervous for her, for the other three guys, and for myself. Hell, I'd be lying if I said it would be easy to say goodbye to the mansion, even if it had been home for only a little more than a week.

Cordy, Cordy, Cordy.

What had he done to all of us?

'Course, he couldn't have known how his little plan was going to throw five people into a state of discomfort and confusion.

"Hey," Brose said, rushing into the room, still wet from his shower. He looked around.

"I thought I was going to be late. Where are the other guys?" He topped off my scotch and poured himself one.

"Not here yet." I glanced at the antique clock on the study's wall. "But I'm sure they will be soon."

"So are we gonna end up with our Garnet, or is she gonna give us the heave-ho?"

There were loud steps in the hallway, and Nat and Linc joined us.

"Hey," Nat said.

"Hi guys," Linc added.

"So, where's the lady of the house?" I asked.

"Right here." Garnet sauntered in, wearing a silky red wrap dress and some out of control fuck-me heels.

Dayum as they say.

She paused and looked at each of us for a moment, smiling. Still, there was something a little sad behind her eyes.

"Look at you, beautiful girl," Brose said with a huge grin. He walked over to her and planted a big kiss on her cheek.

Not to be outdone, I popped up from my chair and kissed her other cheek. Goddamn, she smelled good. Just sweet, clean, woman.

Before I was back in my seat, Linc had pulled her close and kissed her forehead. He stepped aside for Nat, whose mouth landed on hers with a rage that left her teetering in her heels.

I had to say, seeing her marked by my buddies and me like that was pretty fucking hot. My growing cock noticed, too.

Garnet raised her hands up in the *stop* signal.

"Okay guys, okay." Her face was a bright shade of pink.

"I know you all wanted to meet with me tonight, but I wanted to say something first."

We four looked at each other. What was she up to?

She swallowed hard, like she didn't know how to begin.

Looking at the floor, she cleared her throat. "I know I haven't known any of you all that long, but...getting to know you has been probably the best experience of my life. These past days have been so happy for me," she said, wringing her hands.

"Garnet, we—" Nat started to say. But she cut him off.

"Wait. Let me say what I have to. This has been really hard, but I've made a decision. I know what I have to do."

The sadness that had been there before, that I wasn't sure about? Yup, it was real now. I wasn't a sentimental guy, but I could see she was troubled. And I didn't like that. I fought the urge to grab her and tell her everything was going to be all right. It was clear she was working through whatever was going on, in her own way. We had to let her do that.

"As you know, Grandpa—I mean, Cordy—stipulated in his will that I get his estate if I'm married within thirty days. But I can only marry one of you. Because of that..."

I looked around the room, which felt like the air was being sucked out of it.

"...I'm choosing no one."

She searched our faces for reaction, but we all looked at each other.

"But you'll end up with—" Brose started to say.

"No one, and nothing. I'll end up right where I was before all this started. But it's okay. I've made my peace with it."

"Darlin', don't you think you're being a bit hasty? I mean, it seems like there are other options," I said.

"I can't choose from among the four of you. I'm not going to do it. I just can't do it." She held her head up, pretending to be pleased with her decision. But she couldn't fool me. She couldn't fool any of us. There was a heaviness behind her eyes that made even my hard heart break a little.

"I'm giving up the four of you and the money. This has been a wonderful adventure, and I thank each of you for joining me on it. I'm moving out of the house. You can stay here as long as the attorney will let you." Tears welled in her eyes, and I knew it was just a matter of time before they started sliding down her pretty face. Her bottom lip began to shake.

Nat stood from his chair. "Okay. Wait a minute. Garnet, Linc told you we four guys had gotten together and talked the situation through. We'd like to share our thoughts."

Sniffling, she said, "I really need to be going." She took a step toward the door.

"We deserve to say our piece, too," Nat said after her.

That stopped her. She turned around and took another deep breath. Coming back into the room, she took a seat in a cushy armchair and crossed her legs. I know I was supposed to focus on our meeting, but her damn legs were so long and beautiful.

Fuck.

Nat remained standing and turned toward her. "I think I can speak for everyone here." He looked around the room, and we nodded back at him.

"First, we all respect your decision and will support you regardless of what happens. But I think we might have a solution that leaves us all in a better position than what you propose."

She looked puzzled. But she needn't be. We were pretty sure we'd come up with something that would make us all happy.

"We want for the five of us to stay together."

She shook her head slowly.

"Don't worry about the money. None of us cares about that," he said. "Well, I wouldn't say we didn't care, but it's not the most important thing here." More nods.

"Garnet, we want to all live together and share you. We'll find an apartment or something in the city that's big enough for us all. We think it will be the perfect arrangement. You don't have to give any of us up. There won't be any inheritance, but we'll be together."

All eyes were on her as silence filled the room. It seemed to go on for an eternity, at least to me, until she finally spoke. I won't deny it, I was nervous as hell that she was going to shut us down.

"I...I don't know," she said slowly. "I don't know how that would work. I mean, you would *share* me?"

Brose leaned forward, elbows on his knees. "Garnet, I know this is an unconventional arrangement, but Win and I have done this before. You *can* love more than one person. And you *can* make a life with more than one person."

"And Garnet, while Nat and I have not done this before," Linc said, "we think it's a great idea. Speaking for myself, I'm totally psyched. It's fucking hot sharing you, and a relief to me that the other guys will look out for you when I'm on the road for work. Which, as you know, is a lot."

"Yeah, baby, you know I have long, long hours at the gym. I'd feel so much better knowing you weren't being left alone."

The conversation had gotten so heavy, I was determined to lighten things up. "And think of all the fucking you'll get."

That got everyone laughing.

Tension. Broken.

Garnet opened her mouth to say something, but nothing came out. It was just as well. I was across the room like a bolt of lightning, running kisses up her lush thighs.

27

GARNET

Well, I wasn't expecting *that*.

I'd come to the mansion to pack my things, say my goodbyes, and head back to my crappy apartment in the city. I was ending the arrangement and cutting myself off from the guys.

And it felt like I was cutting off my arm.

So when they proposed we all stay together, and to hell with the money, I was shocked. I mean, did they really want to share a woman? Did they want to share me?

Hot damn!

And before I could say anything, Win was on me with his lips, pushing my dress up so he could get at the soft flesh of my thighs.

My nipples jumped to attention and my heart pounded so hard I couldn't hear.

Was I about to have all *four* guys? Like at once?

Yeah, I was nervous. But I was also ready. I wanted them, all of them, right then and there. More than anything I'd ever wanted.

Before I knew it, I was standing so my dress could be pulled over my head, and my lingerie pulled off, leaving me in nothing but my high heels. They led me to a big, soft rug in front of the fireplace. I kissed one guy, and then another. I heard buckles and zippers being opened and a variety of clothing hitting the floor as my red-hot boys disrobed. My head spun as I looked at the Adonises above me, each beautiful in his own way, and each loving me in his own way. Nat with his chiseled jaw and model looks, Win with his wind-swept hair and tan skin, Linc with his broad chest and giant biceps, and Brose with his sexy pierced nipples and neck tattoos—each of them turning me on in a different way. And each taking away my breath in a different way.

And it was all for me.

Fuck the money. Thanks but no thanks, Grandpa. What I found was way better.

Brose leaned over me, and I stroked his brown, bald head. His hands wandered up to my breasts until he cupped my face. Someone teased my thighs, and in the background—I couldn't be sure who—stroked his own very lovely cock.

"What do you say, beautiful?" Brose asked. "I know we've got you at a sort of disadvantage." He looked around at the other guys, and they chuckled.

"But we hope you like our offer," Nat said.

"Yeah, baby," Linc growled. "Are you in?"

Someone's lips were on mine, kissing me deeply, before pulling back and letting me look at each of my guys, one at a time. I'd never felt so beautiful, desired, or hungry for touch. Actually, starving.

"I'm yours," I said, looking from one to the other. "I'm *all* of yours."

"Then lie back, beautiful girl," Brose said. "We're about to make you feel real good."

Eight hands—I couldn't be sure which belonged to whom because I was delirious—teased over my skin. My arms were pulled above my head, where they were held, and my legs were spread wide open as I heard movement and shuffling.

Shaking with anticipation, I exploded in goosebumps. Brose moved aside to let Win kiss me while two other mouths licked and sucked their way across my breasts. I arched my back to give them more and saw Nat nibbling his way up my thigh toward my pussy; leaving me lost in the heat of it.

A tongue—I think it was still Nat's, dragged through my creamy lips, ass to clit and back. I moaned through my kiss and the lips pressed to mine, when Nat moved aside for Linc. His tongue danced around my clit as my nipples were pulled and sucked to perfection.

Every inch of my body was being used for pleasure. The man between my legs, eagerly lapping at my clit, moaned as he pressed and swirled and pressed again. My climax I was helpless to resist.

"Come for us, baby," Linc crooned. "Come on my face."

He got back to work, his face buried between my legs while his hands wandered up my body, sliding over every inch they could reach.

"And then we're gonna do this all over again," Win whispered in my ear.

Someone clamped my nipples with their fingers, and a finger tickled my ass, when a blinding orgasm slammed through me. My screams included the names of my guys while my body spasmed and shook. I'd never felt like that, not even close. Their touches didn't stop, prolonging my orgasm, leaving me seeing spots and gasping for air.

For heaven's sake. Those bastards left me wanting more. Craving more. And needing more.

"I…I want…keep going," I croaked.

"Don't worry, baby," Win murmured as I watched Nat move aside for him.

He was his knees between my legs, hips thrust slightly forward. He spat into the palm of his giant, callused hand and began to stroke himself from root to tip, leaving his precum to drip onto the rug below. Someone handed him condom, which he sheathed himself with in a moment.

"Can I fuck you, darlin'?" he asked. "Can I give you my big, hard cock?"

My head lolled back and forth. "Please. Please fuck me. I need you to fuck me," I begged, knowing the release I was craving, that I would give anything for at that moment, would only come from his cock.

"Yessss," I groaned as he slipped inside me.

His size at first was agonizing, but as he went deeper, I relaxed and moaned for more. I turned my head and opened my mouth, needing someone's cock to feed me, and in a second, salty precum filled my mouth as Win's pistoning rocked me. Another pair of hands held my head, and when Win hoisted my legs higher on his shoulders, I felt one of his thick fingers violate my backside.

Without hesitation, his finger was inside me to the knuckle, doubling the sensation of the dick in my pussy. I released the cock in my mouth and screamed.

"Fuck...yeah...fuck me," was all I could manage. The cock I'd pushed out of my mouth was above my head, a hand stroking it furiously.

"Yeah, yeah...yes..." I screamed, my head and hips bucking.

Win's thrusts were deep and hard, as was the finger in my ass, leaving me wondering if I was about to lose my mind, and thinking I didn't care if I did.

"You're tight, darlin'," Win murmured.

And I began to come. Again.

Hard.

Ripples heaved through me as I was filled and stretched like I'd never been before. They were marking me as their lover. One last thrust, and I tumbled into some place I'd never known, screaming and crying for more. One after the other, they roared as they came either inside or on me, covering and filling me with hot, sticky cum and leaving me weak and mumbling like a lunatic.

"I love you," someone said, starting a chorus of additional *I love you's* that repeated over and over until I couldn't really see or hear any more. They were the last thing I heard from the guys who'd stolen my heart before I passed out, dead asleep.

28

BROSE

Holy shit, it had been one hot night. I'd shared a girl before with my buddy Win, but never with two *more* dudes. Watching Garnet get the working over we gave her just about did me in as I jerked myself all over her creamy tits.

After Win fucked her into oblivion, we carried her upstairs and put her to bed under her fluffy down comforter. She hadn't been kidding when she said she was fixing to move out, because all her stuff sat in duffel bags at the end of her bed. Linc and I put it all back in her dresser and closet to let her know how much we needed her to stay, and we decided Nat would spend the night in her bed while we each retired to our own, spent and blown away by an overload of feeling and sensation.

We didn't know how long we'd be able to stay in the mansion, but for as long as we were permitted, we might as well enjoy it.

The experience gave new meaning to the words *my head was spinning*. I was a cynical bastard, and always figured feelings like that were for softies.

And yet, there I was.

How did I fall for a woman I'd known for such a short period of time?

Next morning, Nat told me he was meeting with Cordy's attorney, someone he'd done business with over the years. Since I didn't have to be at the restaurant until later, he invited me to come along.

It was funny, but with my being a chef, I'd never been in an office like Nat's. He was seriously working for *the man*, but hey, he was good at what he did, and they seemed to pay him well. Seemed a lot more civilized than the restaurant world, and the hours were way better.

"Brose, this is Rick Jones, the attorney representing Cordy's estate. Also a friend of mine from our swimming club."

We shook, with him looking over my tattoos, piercings, and shaved head. It was all good. I told him to come by my restaurant some time.

"So Nat, has Garnet made any progress discussing her financial situation with you?" he asked.

Holy shit. He didn't know Nat was involved with Garnet. He probably didn't know anything about the four of us.

I certainly wasn't going to say anything.

"I spoke with her fairly recently," Nat said, nodding.

Uh, yeah...

"She told us—I mean me—" Nat stole a look in my direction, "—she might be inheriting some money, but that it didn't look like it was going to work out. Something about needing to get married. She said she didn't want to."

Smooth. If Rick hadn't been in the room, I'd be patting Nat on the back.

Old Rick didn't look too happy.

"What?" he asked, his voice rising. "She needs to make that work. What do you mean?"

Nat shrugged innocently. "Not sure, Jonesy. She isn't getting married."

Rick jumped to his feet, pacing to one end of the conference room and back. I wasn't sure, but I think he was mumbling to himself.

Nat looked at me and shrugged.

Jesus, what was up with this guy?

He turned back to Nat. "She has to find someone. Anyone will do," he insisted.

"She has to do nothing of the sort. She's walking away," Nat said.

"Shit. This wasn't supposed to happen."

Nat frowned. "What wasn't supposed to happen? Jonesy, what is going on?"

Rick ran his hand through his hair, becoming more distraught by the moment.

"Cordy..." Rick mumbled again. "Cordy told me she'd pick one of you..."

Oh, shit.

"Rick, what are you saying? What do you mean *one of us?*" Nat stood, hands on hips. He didn't look too happy.

Rick's face turned white as a ghost, then bright pink. I had a feeling someone was in trouble.

He shook his head. "Nat, I'm sorry. I was carrying out the wishes of my client. I couldn't tell you everything."

"Well, it seems like the cat's out of the bag now, so fill us in."

Rick looked from Nat to me and back again. "It was no coincidence that you, Brose here, and Win met Garnet. Linc was a lucky coincidence. You are who Cordy chose. It was up to me to orchestrate the meetings. He thought surely she'd like at least one of you."

He shook head sadly. "But I guess not."

Holy. Fucking. Shit. What a situation. I'd heard Cordy was a little eccentric, but not a mastermind, for Christ's sake. How did he even conceive of an idea like that?

And it was all a set up?

But look at the results. I was in love. Three other guys were in love. And Garnet loved us all. Not such a bad outcome, if you asked me. But Rick didn't need to know the details.

He grabbed his briefcase and headed for the door. "Thanks for the update. I'm sorry to know it didn't work out for you or any of the guys. That's a real shame." And he was gone.

Nat and I looked at each other. "C'mon," he said. "We need to talk to Garnet right now."

NAT PARKED in front of the Drive By, and we ran inside. It was early yet, so we figured she wouldn't be too busy. But even if she were, this was pretty goddamn important.

"Guys!" she said, her beautiful face brightening.

"Do you have a minute?" I asked her. She saw the serious looks on our faces and beckoned us to a corner booth where we could chat.

"Are you guys okay? You look a little pale. Anyway, I'm really glad you came by. I have some good news to share," she said, bubbling over.

"Well, we have something important to share, too—" Nat said.

But she kept talking. "I'm getting married," she said with a huge smile.

Uh. What? Something crashed in the pit of my stomach, and it did not feel good.

"I know, it's crazy. But I'm gonna marry my best friend Matty, so I'm eligible for Cordy's estate, and we'll all be able to stay in the mansion!" She clapped her hands in glee. I was glad she was happy, but I was clearly missing something.

"Matty?" Nat said. "Who the hell is that?"

She threw her head back, laughing. "Matty is my oldest friend."

Nat and I looked at each other, thoroughly confused.

There was a *fifth* guy?

"He's GAY. He's marrying me as a favor."

Oh. Okay.

"He won't be moving into the house or anything. The five of us will still be together."

Suddenly, the news we had from Rick didn't seem so important.

"We're all gonna be together, and I will inherit the estate!" she yelled.

Holy shit. Now that was news.

"Matty and I are going to City Hall this afternoon. I was about to call Mr. Jones just when you popped in. Perfect timing!" she said, glowing.

I didn't know who would be happier—Mr. Jones, or me.

29

GARNET

In the two months since I'd married Matty, inherited Cordy's estate, and moved everyone including myself into the mansion permanently, life had been a complete whirlwind. And it didn't seem like it was going to stop.

I was sad to leave behind my beloved Drive By Saloon, but life had gotten too busy to keep working. So I got Matty's latest boyfriend a job there. My coworker Tom said he was doing great, bringing in all kinds of beautiful women, like gay guys are wont to do, which brought in more straight guys to spend money on beer and mediocre bar food. Something for everyone.

The guys and I still met there for drinks whenever we could, since that was pretty much where it all started. We even fixed a plaque to the bar that said "Bill Cordy Sat Here." Good old Grandpa.

I was so proud of how the five of us were putting

Cordy's money to good use. We had to think he'd be proud, too.

First, we'd started a small charitable foundation to help fund the city's soup kitchens. That was a real dream come true for me, to really, finally be able to do a little something about a problem that hurt my heart every time I saw it.

Linc's gym had taken off, thanks in part to the publicity we got from our charity. He was working long hours and kept promising to hire someone to lessen his load. But I doubted he ever would. He loved the gym too much. Sometimes my hunky man even spent the night there on the very sofa where we…um, well, you know.

Brose was opening his own restaurant in the city, which was sure to be a smash success. He was working day and night, so I'd usually go over there to visit and get some of his great cooking. And, other things.

Nat had quit his job at the accounting firm to serve as CFO for both the restaurant and Linc's gym. No more travel, no more worrying about becoming partner, and no more wearing suits. He still dressed like he walked out of a preppy Ralph Lauren ad though, with his polo shirts and down vests. Such a cutie.

Win was working on renovating parts of the mansion that had gotten a bit old and tired, which Grandpa had never wanted to spend money on. It was going to be more stunning than ever, thanks to my love.

And yes, I was working on becoming a sommelier, and if I played my cards right, I'd be working side by side with

Brose in his new place. In fact, I'd grown so passionate about wine that we'd bought a small vineyard in Napa Valley, an hour north of San Francisco. It would be a few years until we bottled our own wine, but I planned on making it the most delicious in the San Francisco Bay Area.

But the best thing to come out of this crazy journey Grandpa had sent me on was ending up with four amazing guys, who themselves ended up being as close as brothers. It was so funny that Mr. Jones had arranged for me to meet three of them, and that we met in the different ways we had. He told me Cordy had made him swear he'd fix me up with each of the guys. He did his job pretty well, if you asked me. Linc was the delicious icing on the cake.

To celebrate our good fortune, and to sprinkle Cordy's ashes in the Pacific Ocean as he'd wanted, I got everyone to agree to give me five days so I could surprise them with a trip somewhere warm and tropical.

"Hey, bitches!" Matty screamed as he boarded the small jet I'd chartered to take us to the Hawaiian island of Kauai. He wore a huge sun hat and sunglasses with rhinestones. His Louis Vuitton suitcase was so heavy he could barely lift it. Linc took it from him and put it in the luggage closet.

"Thanks, handsome," Matty said to him, batting his

eyelashes. I'd included him in the trip because, well, nothing would have been possible without his involvement. And the guys thought he was a hoot.

"You're welcome, my man," Linc said, smiling.

So of course Matty was invited. He loved the guys, and they loved him back. Well, not in the way that they loved me, but still.

"We're just waiting for Win, and then we can take off," I said.

The pilot and co-pilot emerged from the cockpit. "Have any of you flown private charter before?" the pilot asked.

"No, but we're really excited," I said. Nat and Brose, making themselves at home at the bar, nodded in agreement.

"I'm excited, too," Linc said, looking at me and licking his lips. When the pilots weren't looking, I opened my legs just enough to let Linc see I was wearing no panties under my dress. After a couple discreet glances, he squirmed in his seat, a sure sign he was dealing with a growing erection.

"Sorry I'm late," Win said breathlessly as he boarded. "Hey, darlin'." He bent to kiss my cheek. The pilots looked from me to him, to the other guys. They had no freaking idea what to make of our happy little family and the flamboyant Matty.

The flight attendant pulled the plane's door closed, and we buckled in for a five-hour flight.

***

30

GARNET

Good lord, I'd heard Kauai was amazing, but there was no way words could do it justice. Gigantic palm trees fluttered in the warm breeze, the sandy beaches sparkled, and the air smelled like flowers. Paradise didn't begin to describe it.

And I was in heaven, being here with my guys.

"This is off the hook," Brose said as we arrived at the secluded beach house I'd rented.

I opened the door with the key the housekeeper had given me, and we gasped at once.

The back wall of the house was all glass and overlooked an infinity pool, which overlooked the ocean.

"Oh. My. God." My feet felt glued to the floor, that's how blown away I was. That is, until I heard a small commotion behind me.

I turned just in time to see Nat removing his clothes—

his boxers were the last thing to hit the tiled foyer—and he took off running for the pool. Butt naked.

"Sounds good to me!" Linc yelled, stripping and running after him.

The last two, Win and Brose, looked at each other and shrugged. Before I knew it, they were naked too, and running across the house like madmen.

I looked at Matty, who just shook his head. "I'm going for a walk on the beach. You straight people are just too weird." He pulled his hat low on his face and left us.

Well, who was I to ruin a good time?

I stripped off my clothes and ran for the pool, where my guys were hooting and hollering, and splashing and making cannonballs.

Before I joined them, I watched the scene with a full heart and eyes filled with tears. Funny how life switches directions on you, whether you want it to or not, and when you least expect it. In a few short months, I'd gone from fending off online creeps and their dick pics, to being part of a loving family. We still had a lot to learn about ourselves and each other, but until then, we had each other.

And that was more than enough.

Did you like *The Inheritance?*

Check out the next book in the steamy
Contemporary Reverse Harem Collection
THE RENOVATION

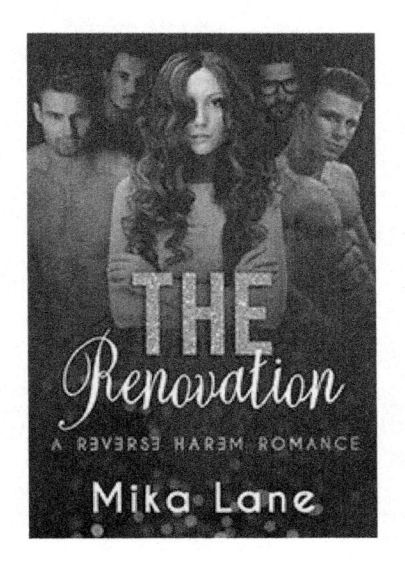

I hope you loved reading this book as much as I loved writing it. Please visit my store to learn more about my books, and to buy directly from me!
https://mikalaneshop.com/

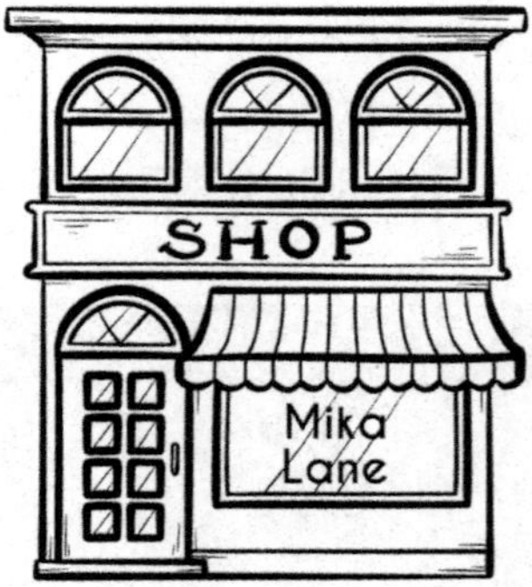
SHOP
Mika
Lane

ABOUT THE AUTHOR

I'm USA TODAY bestselling contemporary romance author Mika Lane, and am OBSESSED WITH bringing you sexy, sassy stories with imperfect heroines and the bad-a*s dudes they bring to their knees. I'll always promise you a hot, sexy romp and my version of a modern-day happily ever after.

Writing has always been a passion of mine (my first book was *The Day I Ate the Milkyway*, a true fourth-grade masterpiece). These days, steamy romance gives purpose to my days and nights as I create worlds and characters that tickle the imagination. I live in magical Northern California with my own handsome alpha dude, sometimes known as Mr. Mika Lane, and two devilish cats named Chuck and Murray.

A lover of shiny things, I've been known to try new recipes on unsuspecting friends, find hiding places so I can read undisturbed, and spend my last dollar on a plane ticket somewhere.

I LOVE to hear from readers when I'm not dreaming up naughty tales to share. Be sure to visit my online shop: https://mikalaneshop.com/ so you know about new books and special deals!

Printed in Great Britain
by Amazon